MONTANA MIRACLE

ROMANCE ACROSS STATE LINES

DEBBIE WHITE

ISBN – Ingram Spark 978-1-955315-09-8

ISBN – KDP 978-1798740811

MONTANA MIRACLE

Editing by Kerry Genova, writersresourceinc.com

&

Leo Bricker Grammatical Eye®

Cover Design by Larry White

Debbie White Books
Summerville, South Carolina

Shelley Bennett held the cup of tea and watched as the little redheaded boy stacked one block on top of another. She held her breath as he continued to tower them, knowing full well it would topple over eventually. His kindergarten teacher, Ms. Marshall, said he was having a hard time learning how to control his frustration, so Shelley was making sure he was learning the right way to deal with his feelings. She closed her eyes for a second. Poor Billy. He'd have to overcome a good many thing. Like why your dad abandoned you at the age of six days, leaving your mother to pick up the pieces. *I mean, really?* How do you ever move forward from that? Shelley had to. It was sink or swim and her instincts kicked in big time. Billy gingerly placed yet another large block on top of the three he already had. It was leaning slightly.

"Look, Mommy." His cheeks blushed a bright red.

"I see. You're doing a great job." She looked down at her phone. "We have to clean up and get ready to go to school."

"I don't want to go," he protested, kicking the blocks over.

"Billy Bennett!" she scolded. "You pick those up right now. That's not how we play with our toys, and that's not how you talk to your mom." She placed her hands on her hips and stared him down.

With his head hung low, he began gathering the blocks and putting them in a giant plastic bag. "I want to go to work with you."

"Next time. Ms. Marshall has many fun things planned for you today. You'll have fun. And when I pick you up, we'll grab a cheeseburger and milkshake for dinner. How does that sound?"

He picked up his head, his teeth showing through his wide grin. He nodded uncontrollably and began dancing around the room. "Burgers and shakes," he sang.

"Go in and brush your teeth. Go to the bathroom, and don't forget to wash your hands."

He bounced down the hall.

As Shelley rinsed out her mug, she could hear him scoot the stool over to the sink to do his business. He painted a ray of sunshine all over her face. He was a good boy. Headstrong sometimes, but a good boy. A tear bobbled on her lower lid. She quickly wiped it away. *No time for tears, Shelley.*

She helped him with his small backpack, which contained a change of clothes and a snack. Then she loaded him into the car. As they drove across town, they sang silly songs to make the trip go by faster. One of his favorites, "Wheels on the Bus," made him laugh so hard he could hardly catch his breath.

As the two came up to his classroom door, Shelley leaned over. "Now promise me you'll be a good boy and have your listening ears on today, okay?" She kept her eyes steady on his.

"I promise."

"Burgers and shakes," she said as she opened the door to the classroom.

"Burgers and shakes," he repeated as he stepped inside.

As he located his cubby to place his backpack, Shelley had a quick moment with Ms. Marshall. "We had a talk. He promised to use his words and also have his listening ears on."

"He'll be fine, Shelley. He's a great student. So smart. He'll go places someday."

"Thanks for saying that." She turned to walk away.

"No, I mean it. I see the potential in him already. He's just a bit frustrated. He doesn't understand a few things regarding his daddy."

"Has he asked about him?" Shelley drew in her bottom lip.

"Yes. Especially when the other kids start talking about theirs."

"I see. Well, he's too young to explain everything to him. I just tell him Daddy went away."

"And that's probably all you can do." Ms. Marshall reached out and touched Shelley's arm. "Have you thought about going to therapy?"

Shelley threw her a strange look. "That's an odd thing to ask."

"I mean, have you yourself come to terms with his daddy walking out on you?"

"That's a bit personal, don't you think?"

"I'm only trying to help. But just think about it. Sometimes it helps to talk it out. And they might have some suggestions for you on how to explain it to Billy."

A loud raucous noise came from the back.

"I do too have a daddy," Billy yelled as he shoved another boy to the floor.

"Boys," Ms. Marshall yelled.

"Billy," Shelley screamed right at the moment he shoved his classmate.

SHELLEY AND BILLY sat in silence in the car. He kicked the back of her seat a couple of times, irritating her even more.

"Stop kicking the seat."

"I'm hungry," he wailed.

She peered at him through the rearview mirror. He tossed her a cheesy grin. "I think you did that on purpose, young man. You wanted to come to work with me, so you started a fight with a little friend."

"He's not my friend." Another kick to the seatback caused her to whirl around.

"Sorry," he mumbled.

"Why, Billy?"

He shrugged.

"I heard what you said to him. What did he say to you?"

"He told me they went fishing. I told him my daddy was going to take me fishing too."

Shelley turned back around and sank into the seat. She drew out her car key and started the engine. "This is not good, Billy. Fighting never solves anything. When we get to the shop, you'll sit at the table and color, look at a picture book, and when I tell you to close your eyes and take a nap, you darn well better do it." She hit the gas pedal a little harder, making the tires squeal. Billy laughed. "It's not funny. Nothing is funny today. Do you hear me?" She held back the tears, but the lump in her throat made it difficult.

Once they got to the shop, Billy hurried inside. He must have known his mom was upset with him. Why else would he run to the small table she had for him and immediately begin coloring? She watched him with a careful eye.

"See, Mommy. I'm coloring. And I'm staying in the lines." He held up the coloring book to show her.

She arched her brow and crossed her arms. "I'm still upset with you."

"I know, Mommy. But you still love me, right?" He never looked up as he painstakingly colored the barn red, his tongue slipping out between his lips as he carefully did his best.

"Yes, I'll always love you."

"You just don't like me right now, right?" His little hand clutched the crayon tightly.

A small gasp exited her lips. She threw up her hand to try to conceal it. She didn't want him to think for one minute anything he did in class today was cute. Although what he was doing right now was cute overload.

"When you're finished with your picture, put a puzzle together. Stay busy and out of trouble. I'll check on you later." She stepped out of the office, pulling the door shut. She descended down the ten stairs to the lower level. The all-glass enclosure that served as her office had a great view of the entire stationery shop. When she had employees, she could let them run the store, and she could do paperwork and still keep an eye on things. But her last two employees quit, leaving her to run the store all by herself.

Rock Paper Scissors was her baby. She started it from the ground up. Bozeman had everything. Everything but a stationery store. So, when the opportunity presented itself, she dove right in. A struggling shop that sold greeting cards, wrapping paper, seasonal gifts, along with a gift registry that was well, outdated, Shelley came in and turned it all around. Along with the usual stationery items, she offered engraved gifts, ornaments from around the world, and unique gift items like globes, trinkets, and even jewelry. Her biggest obstacle was hiring employees. With the low unemployment rate, she was having a difficult time drawing people in to work.

She'd just finished putting up a new display of keychains. She made a deal with the company that if she sold all ten of them, she'd order ten more. She hated the fact she was out an engraver. It would really put a damper on her wedding gift registry. The Help Wanted sign was prominently displayed in the window along with the Open, Come On In sign. She pulled a lint-free cloth from the box under the display case and began to dust the glass tops. She moved to the other counter and did the same. She peered up to the glass enclosure where she got a glimpse of Billy pulling a puzzle box off the shelf. The bell sounded, causing her to look toward the door.

Standing in the doorway, a tall man dressed in faded jeans, a blue tee-shirt, and brown boots, carrying a green duffel bag over his shoulder, smiled at her. His shoulder-length hair was pulled back in a band, and he sported a five o'clock shadow. He took a few steps toward her.

"Hey. Saw your sign in the window."

She blinked. She moved her gaze around his face, landing on his green eyes. She blinked once more.

"The Help Wanted sign." He turned and pointed to the window.

"Yes." Her gaze darted from the window back to him. "Help wanted. Yes, indeed." She clasped her hands and shrugged.

"I'm not from around here. But I guess you figured that out." He tapped the duffel bag.

She raised her brows.

"I got off the bus over at the Greyhound station. I like the vibe of Bozeman. I think I want to hang around for a bit."

"What kind of skills do you have?"

"I spent six years in the army. I know a little about a lot of things." He chuckled.

She didn't know how to break it to him, but knowing how to be a soldier probably wasn't one of the skills she was looking for in her store. "I need someone who can run the register, maybe engrave glass, metal, help with the unpacking of new items. That sort of thing."

"It just so happens I know how to work with metal. I worked in the sheet metal shop on base."

She rocked back on her heels. "But do you know how to use engraving tools?"

"I'm willing to learn. If I can't catch on, you can fire me. I'm used to being fired."

Shelley moved around to the counter. She retrieved an application and laid it on top. "Fill this out for me."

He dropped the bag and came toward her. He took a pen out of the jar filled with rice and leaned over, reading the document. He pulled up from the counter, stuck the pen back in the glass jar, and turned around.

"Where you going?" Shelley asked.

"Back out that door." He lifted his bag.

"I thought you were looking for work?"

He stopped, letting the bag slide off his shoulders.

Her gaze drifted to his shoulders and arms as they flexed, causing her to blush when he'd caught her staring.

"Well, let's see. I don't have a permanent address, nor a telephone number, or a reference, let alone three of them."

"Where do you stay when you're drifting from town to town?"

The pause between them became odd.

"I mean, that is what you're doing right? Moving town to town."

"You were more accurate with drifting. You see, after I spent six long years in a country, fighting the enemy, I returned to an empty apartment. Yep. My wife left me. Divorced me, in fact, all while I was overseas serving my country."

She was shocked. Her jaw agape in disbelief.

He lifted his finger to stop her. "Oh, but it gets better. Then I found out my car was repossessed because she didn't make any payments on it with the money I'd sent her, along with all the furniture we'd bought on credit."

Shelley's shoulders relaxed. "I have a feeling there's more."

"Trust me. There's so much more you don't really want to know."

Shelley looked up to the glass office. She searched for her little redhead peanut, her nickname for him, but no Billy. She put up a finger quickly. "Hold that thought. I'll be right back."

She rushed up the few stairs and pushed open the door. A long sigh escaped her lungs. There, lying on a pile of sweaters she'd neglected to bring home, was Billy. Taking a nap. She quietly drew the door closed and went back to where she'd left the man. The man with no home, phone, and apparently name.

Realizing she'd not gotten his name, Shelley extended her hand to him. A moment later, he clasped her hand and gently shook it.

"Skip Morrison."

"Shelley Bennett."

"Please," she said, motioning toward a stool. "Stay awhile. Let's chat."

He moved slowly toward the chair. "Isn't that what we've been doing? Chatting?" He huffed as he sat.

"I'm good without an address and even a phone number. I guess you could say I like to give the less fortunate a helping hand." Her gaze drew up and settled on his.

"First of all," he said, standing. "I'm not less fortunate. I'm very fortunate. As I told you, I've been where you can't even begin to know how bad it was and have come away able to breathe again and not look over my shoulder constantly. I'm darn happy to be here in the United States again where even though I have nothing, I have everything. Does that make sense?" He spoke without even hesitating between words.

""I'm sorry if I offended you."

"No offense, but Shelley, is it?"

"Yes, Shelley Bennett."

"Shelley, it's just been a struggle, and I'm working through it every day."

"I understand. Listen, if you want the job, you can have it. I might be able to get someone from the high school to teach you engraving. I know the shop teacher."

A slow, easy draw of his lips spread across Skip's face. Shelley could feel the warmth traveling to her cheeks.

"Not like that," she said, pulling up the application and dropping it into the wastebasket nearby.

"Why not like that. You're an attractive woman."

"You're making me blush for real."

"Good. And you're also smiling. Something you haven't done since I stepped in here."

"Well, guess I'm struggling with a few things too. See, I have a five-year-old upstairs sleeping in my office who should be in school today. He got sent home for fighting."

"And let me guess. His dad is nowhere in sight."

Shelley paused before continuing. Was it that obvious she was a single mother raising a strong-willed little boy? She studied Skip hard before she spoke. When was it too much information for a stranger?

"You're right. He walked out on us when Billy was six days old." A tear glistened. "And you'd think I would get used to the idea, but here I am, crying over it still." She wiped the droplets away that ran down her cheek.

Skip moved his hand to the top of the glass display case and rapped his fingers like he was playing a keyboard. Then he slid his hand toward her and turned it, his palm facing upward.

Shelley lowered her gaze to his hand. What was he suggesting? That she place her hand in his? They'd just met. She stood and brushed down her shirt and then stiffened her shoulders, flipping her hair back. "I'm really okay. It's just every now and then I get angry he is missing out on everything. But it was his choice."

"Mommy."

Both heads turned toward Billy. "Yes, dear. Did you have a good nap? This is Mr. Skip Morrison." Shelley turned toward him and tipped her head.

"Hi, Mr. Skip," Billy said as he ran into his mom's arms.

She twirled him around a few times, lifting his feet off the ground.

"You're a big boy. How old are you?" Skip asked.

Now, Shelley knew she'd told him Billy was five. Had he forgotten or was he just being friendly.

"You look to me like you might be six or even seven." Skip grinned.

"No," he said, hiding his face in his mother's legs.

"Well then, how old are you?" Skip persisted with the "how old are you" line.

Shelley pulled Billy back. "Answer Mr. Morrison, Billy." She placed her hands on her hips and smiled down on him.

Billy held up five fingers. "I'm five!"

Skip reared back and laughed. "You could have fooled me. You are so tall."

"I know. My daddy is tall too."

Shelley frowned. There was no way he knew that. She hadn't told him a thing about his daddy. She couldn't bear to even breathe his name, let alone give him any details.

"Billy, why don't you go get your snack out of the bag. I'll be up there in a minute."

Billy ran off giggling.

She turned around after he was out of sight. "Sorry. He's just a little imaginative regarding his daddy. He doesn't know anything about him. If he's tall, short, thin or heavy. Dark hair, blonde hair, blue eyes or brown. I refuse to tell him anything."

Skips gaze looked beyond her. "Well, by the looks of it, I'd say his daddy had red hair and blue eyes."

"And how'd you come to that conclusion?" She tried to wipe off the shocked look that was surely on her face.

"Because you have beautiful golden blonde hair and the prettiest brown eyes I've ever seen. Did you know they have gold flecks around them? They look like little gold bars." He reached for his bag.

She drew in a deep breath and held it. It had been a long time since a man took her breath away.

"So long," he said, giving her a backhanded wave.

"Wait. Don't go."

Skip stopped dead in his tracks and slowly turned toward her.

"When can you start? I mean we didn't quite establish that yet. I can get Quincy to come over and help you with a few classes on engraving. I have a backlog of requests." She shrugged as she clasped her hands tightly.

"Tomorrow. I can start tomorrow."

Her next thought was where was he staying. She knew it was a bit bold, but hey, they'd shared some moments earlier.

"So, where are you staying?"

"I thought I'd find a nice comfy park bench."

His wide smile made her smile back. "No, really."

"I reserved a room at the B and B down the road. I think it's on Cypress Lane."

She twisted her mouth as she contemplated his so-called reservation. "And how'd you do that without a cell?"

He palmed his chest. "Oh, man. You caught me in my first lie." He laughed, then dropped his hand to his side.

She arched her brows while tapping her toe. Maybe hiring him wasn't such a great idea. "Lie?"

"No. Actually, I did have a cell phone. Someone stole it. But at least I was able to make reservations here before they lifted it. You just never know what kind of people you meet at hostels or encampments."

"Encampments. That sounds dreadful."

"It is. Anyway, I can't wait for a hot shower, a nice dinner and clean sheets to sleep in. See you tomorrow."

She blinked a few times as she watched his body move through the doorway. Not only was he a mystery, he was gorgeous, and those two things could be dangerous. She bit her bottom lip and shook her head side to side.

CHAPTER 2

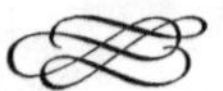

"Two cheeseburgers and two chocolate shakes, please." Shelley spoke loud and clear in the speaker box at the drive-in.

"Fries, Mommy."

"Oh, and a small fry, please."

They collected their food at the window and then drove off. Shelley felt bad for Billy and decided no sense in not providing the cheeseburgers and shakes even though he didn't really deserve them. It was one of her weaknesses. She was constantly making up for his deadbeat of a father. Shelley pulled into the nearby park where children were playing on swings and other equipment. It was a beautiful summer evening, and the temperature remained warm. They found an empty picnic bench and enjoyed their dinner while watching children play.

"Can I go play, Mommy?"

Shelley gazed over at the paper wrapping. One small bite of his hamburger remained. "Sure. But only where I can see you."

Billy jumped off the bench and ran for the slide. Shelley watched as he went up and down it. He never grew tired of it. She noticed the time on her cell. It was beyond bath time for him.

"Hey, Billy," she called, cupping her hands around her mouth.

He looked over toward her, but then ignored her, climbing up the stairs one more time.

"Billy Bennett," she yelled. "Time to go."

He ran up the last few stairs and then slid down the slide, laughing. His rosy cheeks were almost the color of his hair.

"Billy. You must do a better job with listening. When I say it's time to go, it's time to go." She placed her hand on his head and moved him forward.

"I just needed to do it one more time."

"You needed to?" She knitted her brows as they kept walking toward the car.

"Mrs. Marshall said I have a lot of bent-up frustration."

"You mean pent up?" Shelley said.

"Yeah, that."

"So?"

"She said I need to find a way to explode."

Shelley smirked. "I doubt she said that."

They took a few more steps toward the car. She'd already discussed a little bit with his teacher about her predicament. Maybe she was overstepping her authority as Billy's teacher. She watched as he got inside the safety seat and buckled it closed. Perhaps it was time to talk about dearest Daddy even though she dreaded it so much.

"Okay, just a few more minutes in the tub. Then it's bedtime." Shelley began to take some of the toys out and drain them. Billy laughed when she drained a few over his back and neck. He squealed like a little girl, making her laugh too.

She dried him off, helped him into his pajamas, and while he brushed his teeth, she drew down the covers to his bed.

"Read this one, please." Billy handed her a book and then jumped into his bed, pulling up the covers.

Before Shelley was through, he'd fallen asleep. She tiptoed out of the room, closing the door behind her. Creeping down the hall, Shelley entered the kitchen to make herself a cup of tea. Taking in the aromatic chamomile, she wrinkled her nose. Softly shuffling onto the hardwood floor, she snuggled into the corner of their well-worn and comfy couch and put her feet up on the coffee table with the bright yellow crayon marks on the corner. Shelley lowered her head, inhaling her freshly brewed tea. Smiling as thoughts raced through her mind about her crazy day, she lifted her feet and tucked them under her bottom, marveling at the sequence of events and how she made it through yet another day as a single mom and struggling entrepreneur.

AFTER SHE DROPPED off Billy at school, Shelley headed over to the stationery shop. Skip promised her he'd be there. She'd coordinated with her longtime friend Quincy to help Skip with some engraving skills. If everything lined up correctly, they'd both be waiting there for her. She pulled her oversized bag from the car and hung it over her shoulder. It was a beautiful morning. It was hard to hide the desire to flash grins at passersby and return hellos. Living in small-town America had an appeal so many people looked for; it was what enticed her to move to Bozeman four years ago.

"Good morning, gentlemen!" She dug into her fabric bag and drew out the keys to the shop.

"Good morning," Quincy said, puffing out his chest.

She looked up at Skip. "How are you?" She inserted the key and gave it a twist, opening the door. She stepped inside and flicked on the lights. "It's a beautiful morning, isn't it?" She twirled around, her eyes beaming, her smile wide.

"It sure is. I was telling your new employee how we knew each other." Quincy rolled back on his heels.

Shelley's heart began to boil.

"Yeah, he told me how you all went on a blind date." Skip gave her an "I told you so" look that annoyed her to no end.

"It was one date." She held up a finger, smirking.

"It could be a second date if you'd accept my offer." Quincy flashed his fake grin again.

"Okay, let's see." She tossed her purse on a stool. "I'd like you to show Skip how the Dremel tool works. I'm sure he's told you how experienced he is in metalwork. He just needs a fast lesson on engraving."

"It's not something you can learn in one lesson, Shelley," Quincy said, furrowing his brow.

"Two lessons then. I need him on board soon. I have several back orders."

Quincy dug his hands deep into his pockets. "Shelley, I don't think you understand the talent involved in good engraving. One wrong slip and your D could become a P, or your Y could become an X. Do you understand?"

Shelley crinkled up her forehead. "Yes, I do. I'm just panicking is all."

"No need. I also told you that I'd be happy to step in and get all of your back orders filled until you hired an engraver. Do you remember me telling you that?" He narrowed his eyes at her.

"Yes, I recall that. But—"

"I think what she's trying to say, and not doing a very good job at it, I might add, is she feels a bit awkward in asking you to help. She doesn't want to be beholden to you in that way." Skip nodded to Shelley.

Quincy murmured while quickly taking the lead down the aisle toward the back room. "Are you coming, Scooter," he yelled.

"Skip. His name is Skip," Shelley yelled back.

Skip leaned over. "It's okay. We've ruffled his feathers a bit. It's hard on some men when you hurt their egos." He turned away from her and moved down between the lined shelves.

Shelley opened her mouth, but no words came out. Her gaze landed on his back as he traveled to catch up to Quincy. Something about Skip took her totally off guard. Something about how he read her mind scared her, and at the same time, intrigued her.

She busied herself with opening the store, taking a quick inventory of items not moving and ordering a few items she hoped would bring folks into her store. When lunchtime rolled around, she checked on the two men.

"You might make some headway with her, but I sure didn't."

"It's not like that. I just met her. I'm not looking for any kind of relationship."

Shelley's jaw dropped.

"All I can say is if you're lucky enough to—"

"Ahem. I see you two are busy learning the fine trade of engraving." She narrowed her eyes and pitched daggers at them, her blood sizzling about their gossiping.

"Hey, Shelley." Quincy raised his brows then lowered his head.

"He's shown me a few tricks. I think I've got it." Skip reached for a metal sign and held it up. "Notice my *D*." He laughed.

"How about that," she said, directing her condescending tone toward Quincy.

"Well, guess I better pack it up and head on out. I'll come back tomorrow for lesson number two." Quincy weaved his way between Shelley and Skip. "I'll let myself out."

Shelley turned and watched him leave. She counted to ten before twirling back around.

Skip threw up a finger. "Just wait a second. Before you go off half-cocked about what you think you heard, let me set the record straight."

"I heard plenty. He was trying to tell you he hasn't made it to second base with me. But let me tell you, he hasn't made it to first base either and he never will."

"I'm not looking for anything but a job. Trust me."

"Good. Because I'm not looking for anything but employees." She turned on her heels and sped off. "Oh, and that is nice work on the *D*."

CHAPTER 3

Skip couldn't help himself. He watched as her hips swayed out of sight. She was a beautiful woman. Spirited too. Just as he liked them. That is, if he were looking.

He cleaned up the back room before turning out the light. He made his way to the front of the store, where he found Shelley helping a customer. He stood back and waited for her to finish. He browsed the aisle, picking up a greeting card. He chuckled then closed it, putting it back on the shelf. When the bell sounded, and he heard the door click closed, he approached her.

"I'm sorry. It was just locker-room talk. It was never meant for your pretty little ears to hear. I apologize. I should have stopped him, but he was on a roll."

"Apology accepted," she said between tight lips.

He zeroed in on her lips. They made the cutest little bow. "Did you know your lips make the shape of a cupid's bow?" He stepped closer.

She moved back.

"It's kind of cute."

Her hand flew to her mouth as she tried to wipe the bow from her lips.

Skip laughed. "Sorry. Probably too much info. Anyway, the shop is all clean and ready for round two. Have a great evening." He picked up his backpack and slipped his arms through it.

"Wait."

He tipped his head her way.

She shook her head and waved him off. "Never mind. See you tomorrow."

What was Shelley thinking, about to invite him over for dinner? Was she crazy? She didn't even know the man. He was a drifter; he could be wanted for something hideous. Shelley sighed.

It'd been a long time since she let her guard down with a guy. Just ask Quincy. So why the attraction for Skip? She touched her tummy. The fluttering of butterflies kicked into overdrive. Skip Morrison did that to her.

A few more shoppers stopped by, keeping her mind free of Skip. And when it was time to turn the sign to closed one more person entered. The cleaning lady, Jennie Blackwell, came waltzing in carrying a caddy full of cleaning supplies.

"Hi, Shelley."

"Hello, Jennie. How are you?"

"I'm hanging in there."

"Good to hear. How are the kids?"

"Doing good considering."

Jennie had three children, ages three, six, and nine. She'd lost her husband to an accident, leaving her with three small children, no life insurance policy, and only a few thousand dollars to her name. A fighter in her own right, she began to clean offices and shops at night, taking the bus into town because she didn't have a car. It was wrecked badly in the accident that took her husband's life, and even though they had insurance, it wouldn't cover the replacement.

"How many offices are you cleaning now?" Shelley asked.

"Ten. And believe me, I could use a few more."

"Oh?" Shelley cocked her head. "Is it not providing enough income for you and the children?"

"It is, but we need a car so desperately. I've been saving up. I have about five hundred dollars toward a down payment. I just need ten times that amount."

"I see." Shelley took the caddy from her.

Jennie took off toward the back room where the vacuum, mop, and bucket were.

"I'll get out of your hair so you can work. Remember to lock up when you're done." Shelley sat the yellow plastic tote on the counter.

"Okay," Jennie yelled from the back room. "Have a great night."

Shelley gathered her things and then locked the door behind her. She walked the block to where her car was parked. As she put the key into the lock, she just happened to look over the roof of the car. There, Skip was sitting on his duffel bag under the eaves of a store. Twisting her mouth to the side, she pondered what she should do. Then did what any right-minded individual would do.

"Skip," she sang out. "Skip," she repeated.

Skip jumped to his feet. "What are you doing over here?" His skin turned pale while his cheeks turned bright red.

"My car," she said, pointing over to the small blue sedan.

He combed his fingers through his wavy hair and then sighed. "You're probably wondering why I'm out here."

"Sort of. I thought you were staying at the B and B."

"Yeah, well, that didn't work out."

"What do you mean?"

"Remember when I told you my phone was stolen?"

"Yes, but you said you were able to make all of your reservations ahead of time."

"Well, they took my wallet too. Apparently, someone found the wallet, turned it in and the bank put a hold on my credit card."

"Oh, I see. So, the room charge got bounced back. I know Mrs. Ketchum. I could explain."

"No. I'll hang out here for a few days."

"You can't hang out on the corner. The cops will never allow you to camp out here. There's an ordinance regarding homeless here."

With a soft warning he wasn't going to go for that, he said, "I don't want you to do that."

"I know. I can advance you some money," she said, digging into her purse.

He knitted his brows. "I'm not taking your money."

She snapped her fingers. "I've got it."

"No, I'm not coming home with you like some lost puppy dog."

She drew her head back. "I wasn't even thinking about doing that. But I was going to offer the stationery shop. You can stay there until this is all ironed out." She turned on her heels and jogged across the road.

"Come on, I'll go with you so I can explain it to Jennie."

Skip tossed his duffel bag over one shoulder and his backpack over the other. With one hand on the door lever, he looked over the roof at her. "Who is Jennie?"

"She cleans the shop. I just left her there."

Skip slid into the seat next to Shelley. She tore out of the parking lot and pulled up along the front of the stationery shop. She hopped out of the car and motioned for him to follow her. She unlocked the door and poked her head inside. "Jennie. It's me. I've forgotten something."

Skip grunted.

"I mean, I have to leave something."

"Oh great, so now I'm less than human."

She tapped his shoulder with hers. "I didn't mean it like that."

"Hey, Shelley. What's up?" Jennie took the earbuds out when she saw them standing before her.

"This is my new employee, Skip Morrison. He's in a bit of a pickle, so I'm letting him stay here. He'll be up in the office." She tipped her head and looked upward.

"Okay, I finished cleaning it already. In fact, I was about to mop myself out the door." She laughed at her cleaning humor.

Skip took off toward the stairs.

"He's completely harmless. I think," Shelley whispered to Jennie.

"You think?" Her alarmed voice made Shelley shudder.

"I just hired him. He's a drifter, former military guy. I'm training him to be an engraver. But I don't know much about him."

"I'm heading out. I don't want to be tomorrow's news. I have three small children who depend on me." Jennie rushed to the door. "And if you know what's good for you, you'll follow me right on out." She pulled the door open.

She looked up to find Skip looking down. She gave him a quick wave and then out the door she went with Jennie.

She pulled the door shut and locked it.

"You are a beautiful person, Shelley Bennett. You're always thinking of others before yourself. But you also have little Billy to think of. Do you think it's wise to get mixed up with a drifter?" Jennie and Shelley walked the few steps to her car.

"Get in. I'll give you a lift to the next place you're cleaning," Shelley said.

"See what I mean? Always helping." Jennie climbed into the car.

SKIP DUG INSIDE his duffel bag and pulled out an army-green wool blanket and a small pillow with lumps and stains. He made a sleeping pad out of some clothes and covered up with the blanket. A soft glow from the emergency lights inside the store kept the stationery shop from being completely dark. He appreciated that. Sometimes the dark startled him, making his heart race uncontrollably. He held on to the corners of the blanket snugly, drawing it up closer to his chin. Even with the scratchy fabric rubbing against his skin, it offered just enough comfort to soothe his soul. Sleeping with his boots on also gave him comfort and a habit he couldn't seem to break. Maybe in time. Maybe not.

CHAPTER 4

"Billy, time to wake up," Shelley said while opening his closet door.

Pulling his covers over his face, Billy grumbled.

"What do you want to wear today?"

"I don't want to go to school," he said, his voice muffled under the covers.

"Why not?" She sat on the edge of the bed and gently tugged back the covers, exposing him cradling his face in his hands.

"Ms. Marshall is mad at me."

Shelley tapped his leg. "No, she's not. Why would you say that?"

"She said she was discappointed in me."

"Disappointed," Shelley said, correcting him.

"Yeah, that." He rose up and hugged his knees.

"She was disappointed in you because of your behavior the other day, but you've had a good day since. She's forgotten all about it. Now, what shirt do you want to wear?" She opened his drawer that held his tee-shirts.

He climbed out of bed and rummaged through the drawer, dragging out one of his favorites. "This one."

"Okay. Get dressed, wash your face, and brush your teeth. Meet me in the kitchen." She crossed to the door. "And don't forget to brush your hair."

She chuckled as she made her way to the kitchen. She knew full well she'd have to redo his hair, and probably straighten his clothes a bit, but she was trying to teach him good grooming habits. She started her coffee and made extra for Skip. She wondered if he liked anything in his coffee.

"I'm all done," Billy called out.

Shelley's gaze lowered to his outfit. Half of his tee-shirt was tucked in and the other half hanging out. His hair was a bit tousled, and he had toothpaste on his cheek. She licked her finger and cleaned off the white sticky stuff, untucked his shirt, and moved his hair around with her fingers. "What do you want for breakfast?"

He climbed up on the barstool and with both elbows on the counter thought it over. "Pop-tart and orange juice please."

"That's too much sugar, Billy. How about a glass of milk with your pop-tart?"

He nodded.

She fixed up his breakfast and watched him devour his sugary pastry and down his glass of milk, wiping the mustache left behind with the back of his hand.

"Billy! That's what napkins are for." She pointed to the white with blue border paper napkin still folded next to his plate.

He grabbed it and dabbed the corners of his mouth.

She tossed in a bag of bagels she had in the pantry, along with a thermos of coffee and they took off out of the house, giggling.

It was days like this that made it all worth being Billy's mom. He made her laugh, kept her grounded, and at the same time, worried her to death. How could one tiny person have so much control over her life? She lovingly gazed his way, her eyes tearing up just a tad. Her love for him was so deep and never in a million years would she ever understand how his father could walk out on him.

"I'm going to have a great day, Mommy."

"I know you are, and so am I."

"I'm going to have a better day than you," he sang.

"Okay, I hope you do," she said, ending the little good-natured back and forth.

"Will that man be at the store today?" He looked up at her with his vivid baby blues.

In a quick moment, she saw him in those blue eyes. He who chose to be free of responsibility, he who left her destitute and afraid. She gulped. "Maybe," she squeaked out. "Why?"

"I liked him. He said he'd play catch with me."

Shelley parked the car and got out. She helped him out of his approved car seat and took his hand.

"You're almost out of that seat, Billy."

He skipped and hopped while holding her hand, jolting her around a bit. She went ahead and let him get out some of his energy.

"Mommy," he said then took a big leap over a crack in the sidewalk. "Is that man going to be there."

She'd hoped he'd forgotten all about Skip. "When did he say he'd play catch with you?"

Billy hung his head.

Shelley's gaze settled on the top of his little head. She lifted her chin and stared at the classroom door. "Billy," she said softly. "When did Skip say he was going to play catch with you?"

"He didn't. I lied." He rushed toward her, burying his face in her body.

She comforted him by patting his back. "It's okay, Billy. That little lie won't hurt anyone." She tipped his chin with her finger and kissed him on the nose. "Have a great day. I love you."

She opened the door, and he rushed in. Giving Ms. Marshall the thumbs-up sign, Shelley closed the door, walking out into the bright sunlight.

SKIP FOLDED his clothes and put them deep into his duffel bag along with the blanket and pillow. He made his way down to the main level of the store and managed to find the light switch. Running his hand along his jawbone, he felt the several days' growth scratch his fingers. He washed up in the store bathroom, using the liquid soap from the dispenser and paper towels. He dabbed on deodorant and lifting his arms over his head, put on a clean shirt. He finished by wiping down the sink and mirror with his old shirt, making sure he didn't leave any watermarks behind.

When he came out of the bathroom, he bumped right into Shelley. Immediately, she screamed, and he held his hands up in a defensive move.

"It's just me," she yelled.

"I didn't hear you come in. You should announce yourself or something." He shook his head.

"Announce myself in my own store?" She spun around and began to walk quickly to the front of the store.

He followed behind her. "Thanks for letting me crash here." He tried to sound apologetic, but it came out flat and far from it.

"I tidied up the loft and also the bathroom. I'm going to go out and get a bite to eat before I start my day with Quincy."

She unscrewed the thermos and poured a cup of steaming coffee.

"Did you hear what I said?"

She drew the cup to her lips and blew, looking at him above the rim with disconcerting eyes. She put the mug down. "How are you going to pay for your breakfast when your wallet was stolen?"

He pulled out a rolled-up bill from his pocket. "I keep my bills in my pockets."

"I see," she said, her tone holding a bit of "I don't believe you" in it.

"Seriously. I've learned that lesson before. Keep your bills on you. Stolen credit cards can be worked out. If someone takes your cash, well then, you're out of luck. I'll be back." He gave her a backhanded wave and, in a flash, left the store.

He followed his nose to a small diner around the corner. The aroma from cooked bacon led him there. He got a table near the window, ordered biscuits and gravy with a side of bacon, and coffee. He people-watched although it was early and really the only people out and about were those going to work. Some were dressed in business suits, others casual. What was it that Shelley had on today? Oh right. A cute sundress showing off her figure. In daffodil yellow. He chuckled to himself when he recalled meeting her in the hall this morning. He was about to give her a chop, scaring him to death like that. But she'd have no way of really knowing his fears. He never shared them, and he definitely wasn't about to with her.

"Here's your breakfast, sir." The waitress snapped her gum as she placed the plate in front of him. "Anything else I can get you?" Her eyes sparkled, and he knew what the anything else meant.

"Some more coffee." He locked eyes with her and smiled.

She whirled around, her apron strings flapping as she fetched the stainless carafe of coffee.

He ate his food in silence. He had to get a plan together. Get a new credit card, have it sent to the stationery shop, get the B and B reservations resolved, even find a little apartment, if he decided to stay a while that is. He swallowed down the rest of his coffee, dropped the bills on the table, and so he didn't have to have another exchange with the flirty waitress, didn't wait for any change.

SHELLEY TOLD HERSELF, for the first time in her life, she might have gotten in too deep. This guy, Skip Morrison, could prove to be too much. She couldn't save every lost soul. She had her own issues to contend with. Raising a boy to be a man without a father, keeping her business afloat, a roof over their heads, and food on the table. It was a tall order for a single parent. One she took very seriously. She raised her head when she heard the chime.

"Is Quincy here?" he asked.

"Yep. In the back. He can't stay all day."

Skip walked past counter.

"How was breakfast?" she asked as he passed by, smelling like bacon.

"Good." He stopped and turned back around, meeting her at the counter.

"What?" she said, flitting her eyes away.

"I'm sorry I startled you this morning. I'm always on my toes. I never let my guard down. It's the way the army trained me," he said in an unapologetic tone.

"What did you do in the army exactly?"

"Intelligence, surveillance, reconnaissance. In other words, counterterrorism."

"Special Ops?" she said.

"Green Beret." He didn't blink a single lash.

"That's very honorable of you. Thank you for your service."

"Anyway, I don't sleep well at night, always with one eye open, and you might as well also know, I never take my boots off."

"Never?"

"You got me there. Other than showering, I'm always ready to hit the road."

"Have you ever talked to anyone?"

"You mean like a shrink?"

She slowly tilted her chin.

"I'm never in one place long enough to get registered with the VA to obtain services."

"Maybe you can change that. Stick around Bozeman for a while. I hear the people are nice, the air is fresh, and a certain stationery shop owner really could use your engraving skills." A wide smile turned up.

"Speaking of that, I better get to the back room and get my lessons from Quincy." Skip took off down the hall.

Shelley just made the next big mistake she'd always told herself not to make. Don't get too close to the opposite sex. They'll hurt you.

"I THOUGHT you stood me up, Skip." Quincy slid off the stool.

"I was preoccupied. But I'm here now."

"Good. I can't stay long. So, let's get started."

The two men cut out a few sample pieces. Skip enjoyed this aspect of metalworking, and even if he had to pat himself on the back, he thought he was doing a fine job.

"That's awesome. See, Shelley can sell these in the store. People love door hangers with their initials on them." Quincy admired the black metal design with the letter *M*.

"Cutting out metal design is one thing, but there are a few tricks and tools for engraving on glass," Quincy said.

"I'm ready to learn," Skip said.

"Have you ever used a Dremel tool before?" He handed Skip a mask.

"Yes, a heavy-duty one. While I was in the military."

"So, the easiest way is to use a predesigned letter template, but if you must, you can tape on tracing paper, draw out your design and then gently cut it away using a crafting tool like this." He held up the sharp-pointed instrument.

"It can get quite fancy, huh?" Skip crossed his arms.

"I believe Shelley said until she gets the laser machine, she's going to limit it to initials and dates. But once she gets the laser machine, look out. The combinations will be endless." Quincy laughed.

Skip practiced on a couple of cheap glasses Quincy brought. He soon got the hang of using the tool.

"It will just take practice keeping your hand steady."

"Yeah, I don't think she should tell anyone yet about the engraving services. I still need practice."

"Don't worry. I told her I'd help her with all of her back orders until you're able to take it over. I gotcha covered." Quincy slapped Skip on the back.

Skip recalled his earlier conversation with Shelley. He wasn't sure how he felt about Quincy offering his services to her. He already expressed his desire for her. Skip's training told him this guy might not have Shelley's best interest at heart.

"I'm a fast learner, and I'll keep practicing until I get it right."

"Good." Quincy looked down at his wrist. "I gotta get going."

"That's cool. Thanks for stopping by."

The two men walked out of the back room and made their way to the front of the store. Shelley was helping an elderly woman find a gift for her granddaughter's college graduation. She looked up when she heard feet shuffling past her. She gave Quincy a brief smile and then turned back to her customer.

"I'll let myself out. Let her know the offer still stands." Quincy winked at Skip.

Skip walked outside and took in a deep breath of the fresh air. Shelley was right about that. "Listen, Quincy. You know Shelley doesn't like you like that, right?"

He pulled his head back and narrowed his eyes. "Wow. You just come on out and say what's on your mind, don't you? Why don't you also tell me how you'd like to get with her and that's why you don't want the competition."

"Competition!" Skip reared his head back and laughed.

"What's so funny?"

"Dude. I can run circles around you. I can get down on the ground and outdo you on pushups, or any kind of tactical maneuvers you want. She's out of your league. Give it a rest."

"And I suppose the former G.I. Joe is in her league?"

Skip moved quickly and stood two inches away from a red-faced Quincy. Balling up his hands, he bit down on his bottom lip.

"Oh, so now you're going to hit me?" Quincy egged him on.

Skip took two steps back and relaxed his hands. "You're not worth it. But remember what I said. She's not interested. If she were, you'd know it already."

"Whatever." He waved him off and then jogged away.

Skip entered the shop where he came face to face with Shelley. Her crimson cheeks told him she'd seen everything. Maybe even heard too much.

"Can I see you for a minute."

He followed her upstairs to the loft office.

"Where do you get permission to talk to my friends like that, and moreover, treat them that way?"

He couldn't help but smile. She was kind of cute when she got mad. Her bottom lip trembled, and the tips of her ears were bright red.

"I just told him the truth. You even so much as told me you weren't interested in him."

"I told you…it wasn't like that between us. I never said. Oh, never mind. What is done is done. He's not going to come back and finish your training, so now what?"

"I'm trained. I just need to practice. You'll see. I'll be the best engraver Bozeman ever had."

"Is that something else the army trained you on?"

"You bet. You have to have confidence when you're out in the field. You have to have your brother's and sister's backs at all times. War is hell, you know."

"I'm sure." She looked down toward the store.

"Go take care of your customers. I'll smooth things over with Quincy. But I'm telling you, if my gut is telling me right, and it usually is, that guy is not what he seems."

CHAPTER 5

Skip stayed in the back room practicing engraving while Shelley inventoried the new items the UPS man delivered. After she made sure everything was in order, she arranged them neatly throughout the store. No sooner did she get those put up, she had a deluge of people come in.

She joked with the first silver-haired woman she made eye contact with. "Where's the bus?" Shelley laughed.

"Bus?" The woman scrunched up her face, clearly puzzled.

"I just mean, all of a sudden a half a dozen or so people walk into the shop at the same time. It's a strange occurrence, is all," Shelley garbled. "What can I help you find?"

"I'd like to get something engraved."

"Oh? Do you have something in mind?"

"A wineglass. It's for my daughter-in-law's fiftieth birthday."

"That's nice. We can definitely do that. Do you want a stemmed or stemless glass?" Shelley walked her over to the stemware.

Just then another customer came up to them. "Can you tell me where I can find your silver pieces?"

"Sure. What is it you're looking for exactly?"

"A silver platter. I want it engraved."

She paused a moment before answering. Two requests back to back. "Follow me."

No sooner did she get that customer taken care off, out of the aisle came a young woman of about twenty or so, with long red locks, wearing short blue jean shorts, and a red-and-white checkered top tucked in. Shelley's first thought was something from *The Beverly Hillbillies.* "Can I assist you in finding something?"

"Yes, please."

She definitely had nice manners. "What would that be?" Shelley asked.

"I want to get my parents something for their twenty-fifth anniversary."

"I have a chart over here that shows all the traditional and nontraditional gifts for anniversaries." Shelley made her way to the counter up front, picking up a document protector that held the list. "Let's see. A picture frame is one. That would be sweet. You could en—" She stopped suddenly. "Engrave it," she said, finishing her sentence.

"That's what I want. Something engraved."

Shelley dropped the document. She rotated around and looked at all the people in the store. She turned back to face the redhead. "Can I ask you a serious question?"

"Sure."

"Were you told to come in here and ask specifically for engraved gifts?"

"Well, Quincy did mention it."

"Quincy. You know Quincy?"

"We dated a few times."

Shelley widened her eyes then relaxed them. Wasn't he a little too old for her? "I see. To be completely honest with you, I just hired an engraver. He's still learning. This might take a while. When do you need it?"

One by one, when each customer came up to pay for their purchase, Shelley asked them the big question. Did they know Quincy? Every last one of them did. She explained to them like she did to the redhead, it might be a while. She'd just hired an engraver. Then she went to the back room to break it to Skip.

"You know he set me up, right?" He paced the small area.

"I don't know for certain." She cringed. "Okay. I can almost bet he did it on purpose. But it's to get back at me, Skip."

"No, it's to get back at me. He thinks something is going on between us."

Shelley pulled her head back and laughed.

"What's so funny?"

"Us? That's crazy."

"What's so crazy about it?"

"We just met, for one. And, you're not my type."

"What, you don't like strong, good-looking men who served?"

She drew a quick lungful of air and held it. He had a point. "It's not that, Skip. I have my hands full with taking care of the store and Billy. You have your hands full with just living each day. We'd be a mess together."

He stepped closer. She could feel the vein in her neck pulsating. Her hands grew warm and moist. "But listen." She held her hands out as if to brace him from coming closer. "Are you going to be able to do all these engraving orders, or will I have to go begging Quincy to help? Because that's what he's banking on."

"I can do it. I'm more determined than ever, now." His eyes grew dark.

"Not to change the subject, but what are you going to do about your situation?" Shelley said.

"Situation?"

"You know. Where are you going to sleep tonight?"

"Oh that. I was hoping you'd let me crash here again. Just one more night."

"Sure," she said, walking out. "Let me know when you want to start with our first order."

Skip rested his elbows on the workbench and held his face between the palms of his hands. He reared up quickly, brushing his fingers across his jaw and then through his hair. He hated to keep things from her. Especially since she'd been so nice to him. It was hard for him to open up, though. The last time he did that with someone she took his heart, chewed it up like it was steak, and spit it out. He couldn't go through that again. Could he?

Just then, something so powerful came over him like a big cloud on a warm day. He rushed out to see her.

"Shelley," he said, his breath labored.

"Yes?"

"I have to tell you something. I haven't been completely forthright with you."

"You haven't? You weren't in the military, your wife didn't leave you, you didn't get your credit card stolen?" She rattled on before he threw up a finger to stop her.

"Those are all true. But I'm not down and out like I may have portrayed to you. I have money. I have a lot of money, in fact."

"You do? Then why did you want to sleep on the corner?"

"I have some issues. I told you about some of them. I don't like to stay anywhere too long, I don't like to be confined, and well, I like the feel of being outdoors with the wind blowing in my face, the heat on my head, and the soreness I feel on the bottom of my feet by hitting the road so much." He hung his head.

She stepped closer. "Because it reminds you you're alive?" She spoke softly.

He raised up, locking eyes with her. He slowly nodded. "Yes," he whispered. "How'd you know that?"

"Because I feel that way too. I won't even pretend to know what it was like fighting a war, but I do know about broken hearts, and coming home to find the love of your life gone. Sometimes I wish I could run away from it all. But I can't. I have Billy. He needs me more than ever now. I have to stay strong for him. Staying strong for him helps me too. You must do the same, Skip. I already told you, but I think you should make an appointment with the veteran's hospital. Let them help you with some of these feelings. It surely couldn't hurt."

"I think I will. I kind of like it here in Bozeman. I have a really good job and super cute boss. It makes me feel pretty good to be here." He winked at her.

She drew her hand to her face, a giggle escaping between her fingers. She tilted her head a few times. She removed her hand and smiled. "Good. Let me know if there's anything I can do for you."

He slowly made his way back to the work area. "I think I'll be ready to tackle that first order tomorrow. "

"Sounds good. Hey, Skip."

Skip stopped and turned. "Yeah?"

"Would you like to come over for dinner tonight? We're making sloppy joes."

He turned back around and began taking long, steady strides. A big smile wrapped around his face. "That sounds great."

Shelley reached up and touched her face. The warmth radiated to her fingers. Was it crazy to invite him to dinner? Maybe. But he was a lost soul, and in some regards, she felt she was too. Perhaps they could help each other get through the obstacles in their way.

It was hard for her to concentrate the rest of the day. Having him in the back room proved to be a distraction. One she had to learn to cope with. The draw she felt to try to save him overwhelmed her. She wished someone would try to save her. But when she made the decision, against her parents' strong urging, to drop out of college and move in with Billy's dad, her parents pretty much turned their back on her. How anyone could do that to their child, she'd never know. When after she gave birth and it was supposed to be an exciting time for her, she felt the weight on her shoulders of raising a child who'd never know his grandparents. Then when he walked out on them both, she really felt devastated. After she wallowed in her tears for several days and didn't get out of bed for a few more, she pulled all the strength she could muster, packed up the few belongings they had and hit the road. She drove for a few days before pulling into Bozeman. It was so different from Portsmouth. She hadn't planned on staying more than two nights. Just enough to rejuvenate, maybe hang out at the hotel pool for a bit. Try to behave as if they were on vacation, not running from something. But after two days, something happened. The friendly people, the sounds of laughter, the fresh air—it surrounded her, bringing her comfort and joy, and for once, she didn't feel like running.

CHAPTER 6

"Where you going?" Shelley asked.

"I've done all I can do for today. I have a little business to take care of. I'll see you tonight for dinner." He popped a salute to her.

"Wait. I need to give you my address."

"I know where you live," he said, pushing the store door open.

"You do?" She cocked her head.

"The army taught me a lot of things. I know where to find people."

"That's kind of spooky if you ask me."

"It is what it is, Shelley. See you later."

She tied up a few loose ends, waiting for Jennie to show up.

"I'm dragging today, Shelley," Jen said, shuffling toward the display case that served as the counter.

"You do have some dark circles under your eyes. Anything going on?"

"I've been worrying about so many things. It's keeping me up at night."

"Can I help?"

Jen shook her head. "I don't think so unless you have some money laying around you don't need."

"I wish I did. You'd be the first person I'd give it to."

"I just had to pay a pretty high dental bill. Every time I get ahead, something makes me have to start all over."

"I know you were waiting for some financial stuff to go through after your husband's untimely death, did it all come through for you?"

"Most of it. I'm getting his social security now, and his company is also providing some financial assistance. But his funeral expenses took a bite out of our savings account. I'm trying to save for a car, and it just seems it's one thing or another. But enough about me. How are you?"

"I'm doing all right. Business is starting to pick up."

"Great news. I need to find another job too. Working after hours is not working out for us. I get the next-door neighbor to watch the kids, but I feel I should be there with them during the evening hours."

"If my business keeps growing, I could use a hand."

Jennie flashed a smile. "Thanks. I'll keep it in mind.

"I'm off to get that redheaded son of mine."

Jennie moved down the hall toward the closet that kept the vacuum and mop. "Have a great evening," she said, giving her a backhanded wave.

"How'd Billy do today?"

"He did fine. We're making progress. He had a good day, played well with his friends, remembered his manners. I'm so proud of him," Ms. Mitchell said.

"Good. I've had a long talk with him about his behavior. I was hoping it would pay off," Shelley said.

"Mommy," Billy yelled.

"Tell Ms. Mitchell bye."

"Bye, Ms. Mitchell." Billy hugged her.

On the way home, Shelley told him about their dinner guest.

"Oh goodie," he squealed.

"When we get home, you straighten up your room while I get dinner going."

They both dug in and got their chores done. Billy cleaned his room, Shelley did a quickie once-over on the bathroom, hiding the yellow ducky and various other tub toys, gave the sink and toilet a quick wipe, and hung a fresh hand towel.

While the hamburger sizzled in the frying pay, she opened the can of sloppy joe sauce. Just then a knock on the door had Billy running out of his room. "He's here," he screamed.

"Let me get the door, Billy."

"Hi, Billy," Skip said, leaning over and ruffling Billy's hair.

Billy laughed and then ran into his room.

"Something smells good," Skip said, stepping inside the room.

"I was about to butter the hamburger buns." She walked into the kitchen.

Skip pulled out a stool at the counter and sat. "Buttered buns, huh?"

She slathered the creamy butter onto the buns and set them on a cookie sheet. "It makes them better. I do it with grilled burgers too."

"You grill too? I'm impressed."

"I've had to learn to do it all if I want a normal life for Billy and me."

"Are you from Bozeman?"

"No. Portsmouth, New Hampshire."

"You're a long way from home."

"Says a drifter." She twirled around and stared at him.

Slapping his chest as if he were affected by her comment, he said, "You got me there."

"Where are you from?" She turned the question back on him.

"California."

"I've always wanted to visit there. In fact, I thought maybe we'd end up there. But something about Bozeman called to me. I made a command decision to stay put. For Billy's sake." She put the cookie tray into the oven and watched it carefully.

"A command decision, huh? I like that. A woman who knows what she wants."

She pulled out the toasty buns from the oven. "Billy, wash up. Dinner is ready."

"We just serve dinner family-style here. Grab a plate and make your sloppy joe," Shelley said, pointing to the stack of plates, napkins, and utensils.

Skip got up and moved slowly into the kitchen. She watched as his tall and lean presence took up the small space of the kitchen. Billy came running in.

She sat Billy at the table with his plate and a glass of milk.

"Don't be shy. A guy like you can eat two, I'm sure." She giggled, nodding to the one lonely bun on his plate.

He helped himself to a second, heaping the ground beef mixture onto the bun. "I sort of worked up an appetite."

"You sure did. After you left, I got three more orders for engraving. Record sales for one day since I opened the shop four months ago."

"The shop has only been open for four months? I didn't know that."

"When I bought it, it was a struggling store. They basically sold greeting cards, gift wrap, and that sort of thing. I wanted to expand it."

"You'll need to hire another helper if you keep getting business. I will do my best to keep up with the engraving orders, but…"

"No worries. I've already thought about that. If this is just a fluke, then we'll catch up eventually. If it becomes the norm, then yes, I'll hire someone else. I already floated the idea to Jennie."

"It may have been a fluke. Thanks to Quincy." Skip took a bite of his sloppy joe.

"I know you think that, but we don't have any proof."

"I visited him."

"What?"

"Yep. I had to ask him if he was trying to sabotage me. Or you for that matter. Had to get straight with him."

"What did he say?"

"He admitted he'd 'directed' folks to the shop for engraving. To help you out. But when I pressed the issue, he came clean with maybe overdoing it."

With a tone of irritation in her voice, she said, "Just a tad."

"But we got it resolved."

She raised her brows to her hairline. "Oh?"

"Yep. He's going to still direct business to you, but not at the pace he was doing it. And he offered again to step in and help until we get caught up."

"Just like that you're friends now?" She giggled at the idea of him and Quincy as friends.

"Not friends. More of an understanding of position."

"Is that another thing the army taught you?"

A loud crash came. Skip jumped up, knocking over the chair. Billy started crying. Shelley pushed her chair out and ran over to Billy.

"It's okay. Accidents happen."

She ran to the kitchen and grabbed the towel and began to sop up the dripping milk. She looked up at Skip who was running his hand through his hair, clearly agitated by the loud noise.

"Listen, I have to go," Skip abruptly announced.

"You haven't even finished your dinner," she said.

"I lost my appetite."

"Because of a little spilled milk?"

"You don't understand, and you probably never will." He made his way toward the door.

"I might if you let me in."

He shook his head, then left her standing, holding a wet towel.

SKIP STARTED OFF WALKING SLOWLY, then picked up the pace to a full-on run. Breathing heavily, he stopped after about ten minutes. Folding at the waist, he caught his breath. Wiping the sweat from his brow, he checked his pulse. He resumed walking until he made it to the B and B.

Making eye contact with the desk clerk, he took the stairway two steps at a time until he got to his room. After a cold shower, still wrapped in an oversized towel, he sat on the edge of his bed with his face in his hands. Had he overreacted? It was just a glass of milk that crashed on the table, not someone shooting at him. He had to get a grip on this. Maybe Shelley was right. Checking into the VA might be a good idea. He'd become a loner, and it really wasn't who he wanted to be. He loved life at one time. Loved a woman, and would have done anything for her. A crushed heart and seeing the devastation and carnage called war wasn't a reason to hang it all up. It had been a long time since anyone made him think differently. Shelley was that someone. If she'd have him.

SHELLEY TRIED to remain calm and appear as if nothing had happened the rest of the evening. She did a good job redirecting Billy whenever he approached the subject of Skip. But when it was bedtime, and everyone had time to think about the day's happenings, Skip came up again.

"Mommy, why did Skip leave?"

"He wasn't feeling well." A little lie surely wouldn't hurt, she thought.

"I hope he comes back. I wanted to throw the ball around in the backyard."

They'd never even got that far. In fact, he'd only ate half of one bun. She was hoping for so much more. Maybe that was the problem. She shouldn't hope for something that would never be.

"I don't know Billy." She tucked the covers around him and kissed him on the cheek.

She went through the motions of cleaning up the kitchen and then readied herself for bed. But the image of Skip pushing over the chair played over in her mind.

After a restless night, Shelley was up well before Billy. She made her coffee and sat outside, listening to the birds chirping and watching the fluttering of a hummingbird as it drank the nectar at the feeder. She drew the fresh morning air deep into her lungs. The blue cloudless sky brightened her mood, and after a bizarre night, she needed it.

Thankfully, Billy didn't seem to realize how weird the night had really been. Skip running off like some scared dog hearing fireworks. Scared dog. Fireworks. "Shelley Bennett. How could you be so inconsiderate?"

After dropping Billy off at school, she headed right over to Rock Paper Scissors. An apology was in order. Now only if he'd be there—sometimes scared dogs run so far away after a night of terrorizing fireworks they're never to be found. Her eyes glistened with tears as she drove faster to the store. "Please be there," she said under her breath.

She parked the car and immediately began looking for him. She looked on every corner, under every easement, every bench. No Skip. She almost jogged to the store door, hoping he'd be right there wearing a big smile. Who was she fooling? She put the key in the lock and opened the door. She turned on the lights and prepared the store for opening. Still no Skip. She studied the crystal face of her watch. He should be here by now. Her heart skipped a beat. *Maybe he won't come. Maybe he's still running.* She lowered her head and wiped the stray tear that rolled down her face. Just then, the chimes rang. She pulled up her head, flicking away the tear. A bright smile broadened her face. Skip.

"Skip, I'm so happy you came back." She rushed to him.

His eyes never wavered from her. She had to swallow down the growing lump in her throat. She looked down at the old wood floor, noticing the blemishes in the wood that made it unique. He lifted her chin with his finger and drew her eyes back to his.

"I'm sorry I rushed out of the house last night. I got spooked."

"I know. I feel bad for not understanding what you are going through."

He inhaled deeply. "I made an appointment at the VA."

"Good," she said cautiously.

"I want to be happy again. I want to belong again."

His words made her heart ache, and all she wanted to do was hug him. Her pulse hammered, and a tug of emotion squeezed tightly in her chest. She tore her gaze away from the torture.

"Shelley," he said, his tone making the hair on the back of her neck prickle.

She moved closer.

His hands cradled her hips. "I'm not good at this."

"At what?" she said.

"Getting close. But I would like to see where this goes. I mean, if you feel the same way."

She nodded as she stepped closer, letting his arms move up and tighten around her waist, pulling her in.

A small breathless whisper escaped her lips. "I'd like that."

He slid one hand up to her neck and leaned in. His sweet, warm breath lingered above her mouth. She closed her eyes and posed for what she knew would be a nice kiss.

A chime from the door made them both bolt backward. Feeling her face warm up, she turned away and walked briskly to the counter. He took off down the hall toward the workroom. A small giggle gushed from her mouth.

Shelley made eye contact with a gangly looking young man with scruffy long hair, wearing pants two sizes too big. She looked down at his shoes. His big toe wiggled through a small opening. She drew her gaze back to his. "Can I help you?"

"I need a job. I heard maybe you were hiring."

She noticed the yellow flecks around his sleepy brown eyes. She wondered if he was homeless.

"Right now, I'm not hiring," she answered.

"I guess I got bad information." He turned to walk out.

"Wait. Where did you get any information about my store from?"

"Quincy."

"You know Quincy?" She tried to hide the surprise in her reply.

"Yeah. I took shop from him last year. I ran into him recently, and he told me maybe you were hiring a part-time engraver."

She twisted her mouth. Here Quincy was getting all in her business again.

"Oh, he did, did he? Well, I might be looking for a part-time engraver. That is true. So, you have experience in that skill set, huh?" She crossed her arms.

"You can ask him. He said he'd give me a reference."

"Do you live around here?"

"Sort of."

"Sort of?" She knitted her brows.

"Right now, I'm in between places."

What was it with her and Rock Paper Scissors drawing in all the homeless people?

"I'll be right back." She held up her pointer finger.

She quickly made her way to the back room. "Skip," she called. "You won't believe this, but Quincy sent over a young man with experience in engraving. He's looking for a job. How do you feel about that?"

"I could use the help. He mentioned he might know someone. Let me go check him out." He followed her down the hall.

"He's homeless, I think."

"Why do you think that?"

"You'll see. Besides, he told me he's 'in between' homes.'"

"Ahh. Got it."

"Hey, Skip Morrison," he said, extending his hand to the young man.

"Damian Porter."

"Good to meet you. So, you're inquiring about the engraving position?"

"Yeah. Quincy said you might need some help."

"Gotta get the okay from the boss." Skip turned with his arms crossed, his pleading eyes softening her heart by the second.

"Sure. Let's give it a try." She reached under the counter and produced a document much like she'd asked Skip to fill out initially. "Just fill out what you can."

"When you get done with the paperwork, come on back and see me." He mouthed *thank you* to Shelley and disappeared down the hall.

"Here you go," Damian said, sliding the one-page application across the counter.

She quickly glanced at the space for a phone number. She nodded. "Good deal. I have a number to reach you at. Go ahead and go back and see Skip. Down the hall," she said, motioning with her head.

"Thanks again. I appreciate it."

"Sure. I don't know how many hours I can give you. But hopefully, it will help." She looked away for a second before looking again toward the back room. She hated that she didn't completely trust him. Maybe Skip would find out the real story and share it with her.

SHELLEY POKED her head inside the back room after Damian left. "Well?"

"He's good. He's got some mad engraving skills. You'll be happy you hired him." He stood.

"Jennie comes in tonight to clean the building. I'm getting ready to leave."

"Okay. I'm almost done. I just want to finish these wineglasses." He picked one up from the workbench.

"Wow. That is so pretty," she said, her eyes making contact with his. She cleared her throat. "Anyway, have a good evening. You're at the B and B, right?"

"Yep. See you." He turned back to the Dremel tool.

"Good night."

"Night."

She began to close the door, and when it was ajar, she swung it back open. "We have to talk about the kiss."

He whirled around on the stool, his stare deep and alluring. "The kiss that got away."

"Yeah, that one." She gulped.

He slowly eased toward her. She couldn't help herself. Her gaze darted down and up his entire frame and landed back on his face. The thumping in her ears drowned out any other noise, if there were any. And as if in slow motion, he reached for her and pulled her in. She didn't resist at all. This was, after all, what she wanted, right? He wrapped his arms around her waist and held her.

Their eyes never dithered from each other. Steady as a steel pole, they latched onto one another as if their life depended upon it. Maybe it did.

"You see, I was hoping we'd have another opportunity. And we are." He swayed and dipped her in his strong arms, making her blood heat to almost boiling.

An answer crept out, almost a hoarse whisper. "Skip."

He lightly touched her lips with his fingers. "Don't say anything." He leaned in and was about to give it to her when Jennie hollered, "Shelley. It's me. Anyone here?"

She drew back out of his arms. "Jennie."

He rubbed his chin. "The cleaning lady?"

"We'll have to table this for another time." She rushed out of the room, closing the door loudly behind her.

"Jennie," Shelley said, out of breath. "You're early."

Jennie looked at her watch. "No, I'm right on time. You're late. What are you staying behind so late for? You're normally out to get Billy."

Skip came up behind them, startling Jennie. "Ahem."

"You remember Skip Morrison. He's my engraver." Shelley refused to make eye contact with Jennie.

"Yes. Nice to see you again," Jennie said.

"I'm off to get Billy," Shelley announced. "See you later, Jennie. See you tomorrow, Skip." She grabbed her bag and rushed out. When she got in her car, she started laughing uncontrollably. She reared back and leaned against the headrest. She felt like some schoolgirl with her first boy crush. Skip Morrison had this effect on her. "Crazy stuff happening right here," she said out loud.

"I HOPE I didn't interrupt anything?" Jennie uncoiled the cord to the vacuum cleaner.

"No, not at all. I just started here a few days ago. We hardly know each other."

"I see. Well, I thought I detected a bit of awkwardness." She plugged the machine in.

"I'm leaving now. Have a good evening," Skip said.

"Good night." She turned on the vacuum and began pushing it.

Thankful for the noise of the vacuum, Skip took off for the B and B. If Jennie could sense something between them, then that meant it was obvious. Shelley had a hold of his heart, jumbled up his feelings, and made him not know if he was coming or going. All he could think of was her cherry-red lips, gorgeous brown eyes and long black lashes, and the smallness of her waist when he held her in his arms. He shook off the thoughts. Maybe it was too soon?

Shelley picked up Billy from the after-school program. She tried hard to pick him before the teachers walked them over, but with the swinging door of customers and the new hire, she never made it to the school. Billy looked forward to hanging out in the loft office, drinking his apple juice through a straw and munching on his crackers shaped like fish.

"Mommy. You're late." He crossed his arms and pouted.

"I know, dear. I'm sorry. Mommy had a lot of people come into the shop today."

"Burgers and milkshakes?" He crossed his arms tighter and dropped his chin.

"Sure!"

"Yeah!"

"I have one little stop to make, first," she said, belting him into his booster seat.

She waited in her car until she saw his head bobbing through the row of cars. It was still warm outside; the heat index had been quite high. She ran the air conditioning to keep her and Billy comfortable while she waited. She popped the door open and jumped out.

"Jeez, Shelley. You scared the *you know what* out of me," Quincy said.

"Sorry. I've been sitting in my car waiting for you."

He peered over to the running car. "Billy inside?"

"Yes. I won't be long. We're on our way to get burgers and shakes."

"It's a good day for milkshakes. It's hotter than a blue blaze."

"I'm not here to talk about food or the weather for that matter. Don't send me any more homeless people to save. Got it." She turned back toward her car.

She stopped when she felt his hand on her shoulder. She shook it off and turned to face him. "Don't touch me."

"I was trying to help Damian. If you can't use him, then let him go."

"What's his story?"

"He took four years of shop with me. He's super talented."

"No, I mean his other real story. Why is he homeless?"

"Oh that. Well, his parents moved to California after he graduated. Which by the way, he graduated at the top of his class."

"Go on." She tapped her foot. "I don't have all day." She tiptoed to see Billy's head. He was amusing himself with a book.

"They got burned out of their house during those awful wildfires. They became penniless and homeless overnight. He got tired of living in shelters, so he came back to Bozeman."

"To live in more shelters?" She tilted her head as she tried to make sense of it all.

"I guess he thought it would turn out better than it did. He needs a good job and then he can get a roof over his head. He's been doing odd jobs. He saved up enough to get the cell phone, and he can eat out occasionally."

"He seems like a nice kid. Okay, gotta run." She put her hand back on the door lever. "But I mean it, Quincy. No more helping me. No more customers, no more hired help."

"How about a date then?"

She dropped her shoulders and shook her head. "Don't you get it? I'm not interested. Never will be. Go find someone else who will fill your needs."

"Because you found someone to fill yours?"

His bold statement took her by surprise. She pulled open the door and slid into the seat. Peering into the rearview mirror, she watched as he strode by her car, a cocky grin plastered on his face. The nerve of him. Where did he get off examining her feelings? She popped the gear into reverse and tore out of the parking lot.

"Burgers and shakes," Billy sang.

Flying out of the parking lot, Shelley's brain was the consistency of mush. Her thoughts boomeranged from one side of her soft tissue to the other. The rapid beating of her heart along with sweaty palms made gripping the steering wheel a bit of a challenge. Was Quincy, right? Deep down inside, she knew all along he was. When would she let her guard down and let Skip in? Really let him in?

Shelley attempted to walk inside the burger joint, but her legs were heavy. It felt like someone had dipped her shoes in cement. The fuzzy feeling inside her head made giving the order to the clerk almost impossible. She rambled their order off like a bumbling idiot. Thankfully, it was a young teen working the register, and he didn't even notice.

She carried the tray loaded with burgers, fries, and two milkshakes and led the way to a table far in the corner. As she and Billy ate their dinner, Shelley made small talk with her son, but the truth of the matter was, she was consumed with Skip. Every inch of her brain held a little piece of him. How he looked, how he walked, how he talked, how his earthy scent followed her everywhere. She shrugged. It was no use. *Eat the burger, Shelley. You're too much of a mess right now to be anything else but an eating machine.* So, she took a big bite and then another.

SHELLEY WATCHED her cell phone like a hawk watches a field mouse. She sighed, crossed her legs, then sighed again. She uncrossed her legs, set deep back into the cushion, curling her legs underneath. After a few minutes, she looked at the phone again. "I know he has a phone. I wonder why he won't call me?"

"Mommy. I'm ready for my bedtime story."

She tucked her phone in her back pocket and shuffled into his room. He'd already picked out his book. She sat on the edge of the bed and went through the motions, but when it got to be too much, she abruptly stopped.

"Mommy, why did you stop?"

"I'm just feeling a bit sad tonight." She patted his leg and then resumed reading.

When she finished the book, she kissed him on the forehead, turned out the light, and closed the door slightly. She moved to the kitchen and rinsed the dinner dishes, stacking them in the dishwasher. She wiped down the counter with kitchen spray, then, like a defeated ballplayer, headed to the showers with her head bowed. Her phone started ringing and vibrating in her pocket.

She tried to yank it out, but it wouldn't cooperate. Finally, she pulled it loose. "Hello?"

"Hey. I didn't catch you at a bad time, did I?"

She sat on the edge of her bed, bouncing a little. "No, not at all. In fact, I just finished tucking Billy into bed."

"Good. I tried to time it when I thought he'd be in bed. I know you all have your routine," Skip said.

"Yeah, that we do. Children like routines." She shook her head and grimaced at her strange reply. "But hey, how are you?" She quickly changed the subject.

"I'm good. I wanted to ask you something."

"Okay. I'm all ears."

"Would you and Billy like to go on a drive up through the Bridger Range?"

She paused momentarily. Seemed odd to get invited on a drive when you didn't own a car. "I guess. Yes, sure. Billy would love that. I just got my car serviced, so we're good for a long trip through the winding mountains."

"We don't have to take your car. I bought one," he said.

"You did?"

"Yes. Tonight"

"You had a driver's license all this time?"

"I never said I didn't."

"I just assumed—"

He cut her off swiftly. "Just assumed because I was a drifter, I didn't have any identification? I also have a military ID."

"Your wallet…"

"They were stolen, too, but I got replacements. I took the bus over to Malmstrom Air Force Base, and they hooked me right up with a new ID card. Then I braved the department of motor vehicles in Bozeman and got a new driver's license."

"Did you have to retake the test?"

"Just the written and eye exam. Piece of cake."

"What kind of car did you get?"

"Actually, it's a truck. You'll see it. I'm driving it to work tomorrow. We can discuss the trip then. I looked ahead at the weather for Saturday, and it's going to be awesome."

"Sounds good. I'll pack a picnic lunch for us."

"Hey," he said, his voice low with a hint of huskiness that made the hairs on her arm crawl.

"Yeah," she replied.

"I don't know if I told you or not, but thanks again for taking a chance on me. I really needed a place to hang my hat for a while. It gets lonely out there."

"You mean, you crave routines too?" She snickered, trying to break the seriousness of their conversation.

"I think I do."

"Well, I'm glad you walked into my shop that day. See you tomorrow."

"Good night, Shelley."

"Good night."

She rolled back onto the bed, her legs hanging off. She tossed the phone next to her and closed her eyes. "He likes us, Billy," she whispered. A tear trickled down her cheek.

CHAPTER 8

Her heart fluttered, and her tummy rolled and knotted in anticipation of their meeting after the somewhat flirty phone conversation the night before. When he bounced through the door to the shop with a smile as wide as he could possibly stretch his lips, his eyes sparkling and dancing along with his hands wailing, she figured he must have been also anticipating their exchange this morning.

"Good morning," he sang.

A warble of a chuckle escaped her mouth. She quickly threw her hand over her mouth to hide the humor.

"It's going to be a beautiful day," he said, nodding.

"Yes, it is," she said, unsure of what to say.

"I'm going to finish the orders from last week. See you later." He headed down the hall toward the back room.

"Hey, Skip." She turned around.

He stopped and faced her.

She crossed her arms and hugged them. "Never mind." She raised up on her toes, finally rocking back on her heels. "Have a good day."

"See you around lunchtime." He sped off.

She turned back around and began putting the cash from the safe into the register. Having a good day seemed the only possible outcome. Skip brightened her day, made her feel alive again. "I wonder if he likes turkey or ham," she pondered as she began to make a mental list of the picnic items.

"Good morning, Shelley," Damian said, rushing in past her.

"He's waiting for you," she called out as he ran by.

Could this day get any better? It just may, she mused.

And it did. A steady stream of customers came in throughout the day. She sold greeting cards, stationery, colored pencils and sketch pads, a set of crystal birds, and a purple bud vase. She took orders for custom engraving, made suggestions for gifts, and she took a couple of special orders. Turning the Closed sign on the window, she hobbled slowly back to the stool. Slipping her shoes off, she leaned over, rubbing the balls of her tired feet. How she dreamed of soaking in a tub of bubbles.

"Good night, Shelley," Damian said, flipping up a wave.

"Good night, Damian. Have a good night."

"Hold up, Damian," Skip called, jogging up behind him.

Shelley watched the interaction between the two. Skip talked low so she couldn't hear every word. Then he patted Damian on the back, and the two walked out.

She slipped on her shoes. She moved toward the register to cash out and get the money counted when Skip appeared.

"I almost forgot to say good night."

She tossed him a flirty smile. "No worries. Seems you had other stuff on your mind."

"No, not really." He looked back over his shoulder. "Well, I'm going to help out Damian. He needs to get out of the shelter and off the streets."

"That's very kind of you. I was trying to think how I could help him too. Maybe advance him his pay for the week?" She counted out some bills and slid them across the counter. "Here, give this to him."

Skip shook his head vehemently. "No, I'll loan him the cash." He tapped the bills and then slid them back toward her.

She picked up the bundle. "Are you sure?"

"Yep. And listen, I also didn't forget about our ride and picnic. We were busting out the jobs back there today. We're caught up."

"I know. That's good news because I've taken a few more orders today." She lifted her shoulders to her ears, raising her brows.

"We're still on for Saturday. I haven't forgotten."

"Okay. Do you like turkey or ham?"

"Yes," he said, with a cheesy grin.

She burst into a smile. He made her feel funny inside, and she loved it. "I'll surprise you."

"See you tomorrow. TGIF," he hollered.

Jennie almost collided with him as she ducked under his arm and threaded through the door opening.

"He's in a terrific mood," she said, putting her cleaning supplies down.

"I'm glad. He has a lot of baggage."

"I thought so. What kind?" She leaned on the counter with her elbows, listening intently.

"Jennie!" she said.

"Let's see. His wife left him and broke his heart, he lost his job, filed for bankruptcy, and she never lets him see their kids?"

"Not exactly," Shelley said.

"Not exactly. Hmm. So I'm close."

"He is a veteran. Army. While he was away, his wife left him. He came home to an empty apartment. Everything he owned was repossessed because she didn't keep up with the payments while he was deployed. He's wounded, but he'll survive. I know it right here." She rested her hand over her heart.

"I thought I didn't interrupt anything the other night?" Jennie said accusatorily.

"I like him. I like him a lot. And he likes us."

"I'm happy for you. I really am."

"Enough about me. How are you and the children doing? Any closer to getting a car?"

"I had to spend all of the money I had saved as a down payment for Lacey's braces."

Shelley hung her head.

"But don't you worry about us. We're doing okay. Kids are adjusting, I'm hanging in there, and I'm so thankful and blessed to have a job."

"I just hate that you have to ride the bus," Shelley said.

"It could be worse."

Shelley cocked her head.

"We might not have a bus service. Then what? I'd have to hoof it. Now, that wouldn't be nice." She walked off.

SHELLEY COULDN'T HIDE her disbelief when Billy came running out of his room wearing red shorts, a green shirt, and blue socks.

"I'm ready to go on a picnic," he said, jumping up and down.

"I see." Her gaze lowered to his blue socks.

"Maybe we should change some of your clothes." She wrapped her arm around him and led him back into his room.

"I like these clothes," he said.

"I like them too. But just not together." She pulled him close.

After she helped him find a coordinating shirt and change to white socks, Shelley finished putting the picnic items in the basket. She'd made hoagie-style ham sandwiches, deviled eggs, and Billy insisted on potato chips. She filled a gallon jug with lemonade and chucked it full of ice to keep it cold. She packed a blanket, some napkins, paper products, and a few bottled waters, in case the sweetness of the lemonade made their mouths pucker.

A light rap on the door caused Billy to rush toward it.

"Wait," Shelley yelled.

He stomped his feet, then crossed his arms.

She peered into the peephole.

"Okay, you can open it."

He pulled the door open and leaped into Skip's arms. "Hey, Skip."

Skip's quick movement caught him, and he pulled him straight up and then looped his legs on each side of his head.

"Someone is so excited about our road trip today."

"Good." He glanced over to the basket and large, stuffed bag.

Skip moved toward the basket and laced it through his arms. Shelley couldn't help but stare at his bulging arms, and the apparent strength he had. He had Billy over his shoulders, the heavy basket on his arm. She grabbed the bag.

"And, we're off," Skip said as he galloped out the door, making Billy laugh.

The ride started out a bit tense. She didn't know how to start the conversation off and apparently neither did he. Finally, she broke the silence.

"Billy brought some binoculars. He said we might see some bighorn sheep."

"That's a big possibility," Skip said.

"I made deviled eggs. I hope you like them."

"Are you kidding? I love deviled eggs."

"I also made lemonade." She shrugged then looked out the window.

"Love lemonade too."

He moved his hand to the radio and turned the volume up slightly. "How do you like my truck?"

"Oh, I love it," she answered, glad for the conversation to move away from food.

"I got a great deal on it. It only has twenty-two thousand miles on it. Just broken in actually." He flashed her a smile, making her heart melt.

"Good. That's really good." Her gaze focused on his plump mouth and chiseled jawline. She drew in her bottom lip and bit down. He was so gorgeous. She let out the held breath slowly.

He drove cautiously around the curves, and she appreciated that. A safe driver with her most precious asset sitting in the back seat, looking out the window with his camouflage hat and binoculars pressed to his face. A warm smile crossed her face. Nothing like a love for your child. Just then, an image of her parents flashed before her.

"So, isn't this beautiful?" She let out a long sigh.

"Yes. The wildflowers are popping with color," he said, pulling off to a lookout point.

They got out and took pictures and watched Billy as he tried to find anything of interest with his binoculars.

They drove about an hour more before they found another turn off with picnic tables. "Let's have lunch here," Skip said.

Shelley laid out the paper plates, napkins, and cups. "Lemonade?" She pulled the plug to the red-and-white jug holding the sugary water drink.

"Fill'er up," Skip said, holding his cup high.

"Fill'er up," Billy echoed, holding his cup up.

The yellow drink gurgled as it flowed out of the hole and into their cups. An ice cube plopped out, splashing the lemonade. Billy laughed.

Shelley and Skip chattered up a storm about everything. From how delicious the lunch was to the scenery of their trip.

"I'm done, Mommy. Can I go exploring?" Billy hopped down off the bench.

"Yes, but stay right here. Don't wander off."

She leaned her elbows on the tabletop, her hands holding her face as she listened to the story about how Skip wheeled and dealed for his truck.

Skip leaped from the bench and slid across the top of the table. Shelley shrieked as she moved out of the way. When she heard Billy cry out, she whirled around, leaping up herself. Skip tossed Billy over to her. He pulled the knife out of the sheath on his hip, and Shelley turned Billy's head away. They both stared off into space.

"It was a big snake, Mommy."

"It was. I told you not to go too far. You must listen to me."

"I saw a pretty rock and some flowers."

"Unfortunately, the snake was living near them," Skip said, slipping the knife back into the leather holder. "I hate to kill snakes out here. This is their house. But it got just a little too close for comfort."

"What kind was it?"

"Prairie rattlesnake. Very venomous."

Shelley held Billy tight.

THINGS COULD HAVE GONE bad out there. Skip stayed focused on the road. That rattlesnake was too close for comfort. They were so far away from any hospital too. He raised his head and peered into the rearview mirror. Billy was playing with a handheld electronic game. He turned toward Shelley. She looked especially pretty today. The outdoors brought a warm blush to her face, and a glow to her hair, giving it highlights he'd not seen before. And the light floral scent that wafted in the cab of his truck awakened his senses and made his pulse kick up a notch or two. Being with her made him feel light and happy. Some days could be so dark and heavy. This was a great change for him. One he welcomed.

"I'm glad we did this." He twisted slightly, hoping she'd look his way.

"Me too. It was so nice. Thanks for thinking of it." She blinked a couple of times, batting her long lashes.

"I love to just drive. It beats walking." He laughed at his own joke.

Gasping, she blurted, "Speaking of that. I'd really like to help Jennie out. She's been saving up for a down payment for a car and instead had to use it for her eldest daughter's braces. She takes the bus to town every day to work and to run errands. God forbid if one of those kids gets sick."

"Why is she without wheels?" Skip asked.

"Her husband was killed in a tragic car accident. Their car was totaled. The car insurance didn't cover it all. They didn't have a lot of money saved up and unfortunately no life insurance policy either."

"Wow. That's messed up."

"She is super sweet. I'd love to help her some way."

"Do you have an idea how we can help?"

"She won't take charity. I know that much," Shelley said, drumming her cheek with her finger.

"How about a fund-raiser?" Skip asked.

"That might work."

A tug of emotion squeezed his chest. Showing a momentary flash of empathy, he said, "You come up with the plan, and I'll make it happen."

fter he dropped them both off, safe and sound, he drove back to the bed and breakfast. The clerk flashed him a quick smile and went back to reading a magazine. He took the steps to the second floor and entered his room. He'd paid for three nights for Damian and wondered if he was back in the shelter, or worse, on the streets now that he had to check out. Kids like him were street-smart though, and Skip knew enough to not crowd him. He'd bolt if he felt smothered.

Still full from the great lunch Shelley prepared, Skip showered and changed and headed out on the town. There was only so much of staying inside trucks and boarding rooms he could take. Walking the sidewalks helped him relax and get his head back on straight. Tomorrow was his first appointment with the shrink. A little anxious of how it would all go down, Skip stopped into the local watering hole and grabbed a frothy cold one. He found a table in the corner and sat listening to some loud-mouthed tourists talking about their outings, a group of locals shooting pool, and the lovers in the opposite corner smooching the night away. Skip sipped his beer and watched the world.

He wiped the foam from his mouth. The image of the big snake so close to Billy caused his skin to crawl. Shelley's scream still echoed in his head. A flashback to another time stirred up deep within him. He drew the mug to his mouth and drank. Maybe this staying put in one place was a bad idea.

STILL SHAKEN by the day's events, Shelley dug out the bottle of amber liquid and blew the dust off. Drawing open the cupboard, she retrieved a small glass. The alcohol warmed her insides as it traveled deep into the pit of her stomach. She shook off the aftertaste and took another gulp. Being a mom was hard enough. Being a single mom, well, that was brutal. No one to bounce anything off of, no one to tell your deepest fears to about parenting. She sighed. She downed the rest of the drink and put the bottle away, where it would stay for hopefully months.

"Mommy, I'm ready for my bedtime story."

She drew in a deep breath and squared her shoulders. Flipping her hair back off her, she yelled back, "Coming, dear. I'll be right there."

Shelley took the colorful book out of Billy's hands. "Again?"

He loved the book about the little boy who visited his grandparents' farm.

"I love that story." He beamed with joy as he snuggled under the covers, ready for his story.

Shelley went through the motions of reading the book, trying to make it light and funny, but truthfully, she felt a bit uneasy after today's close call.

When she finished the book, she sat it on the corner of his nightstand. Pulling the covers up closer, she leaned over and kissed him on the cheek. "Did you learn anything from today, Billy?"

"Yes, Mommy."

"What?" She wanted him to answer her.

"Not to go too far. Put my listening ears on."

"That really scared Mommy today. I don't know what I would have done if that snake had bitten you."

"I do, Mommy." He pushed the covers down and sat up.

Shelley narrowed her eyes.

"Skip would have rushed me to the hospital. He would have saved me." He patted the bedspread and then clapped in excitement.

"Maybe. But please be more careful. Look, listen, and be aware."

"Okay," he said, burrowing under the covers.

WITH THE FLOOR light in the corner on, the living room was dimly lit, casting a soft shadow. Shelley sat on the sofa while resting her feet on the coffee table. Just then, her phone rang. She quickly answered it before it woke up Billy.

"What are you doing?" Skip asked.

"Sitting here thinking about today."

"Yeah. That's all I can think about too."

"We talked about it tonight after a bedtime story. I think he understands more now. But I guess being a mother will never stop me from always worrying about him." She crossed her feet at the ankles and wiggled her feet.

"I'm just glad I was there. It could have been so much worse."

She let his last few words soak in before answering. "True. I do realize that. I guess I was preoccupied."

"With me?"

She pursed her lips, pausing again before answering. "I think so."

"You think so?" he pressed.

"Yes. It was you. I haven't had a male friend to talk to in a long time. And before you bring him up, that includes Quincy."

"I wasn't going to bring him up."

"You weren't? Hmm." She laid her head back on the sofa, her head settling into the cushion, and looked at the ceiling.

"Okay, I was going to bring him up," he said.

"Yeah. I thought so. Anyway, I took my eye off the ball."

"Oh. I like the sports parallel. Catchy."

Laughing, they both said at the same time, "Another sports analogy."

"What are you doing tonight?" she asked.

"Sitting in a dark corner, drinking a beer."

She nodded, fully aware he couldn't see her response. She wondered if she should share with him her earlier indulgence. She watched intently as the darkness outside loomed, making the dimly lit room even darker. She pulled up from the couch and went over to the glass slider, closing the drapes. She switched on the kitchen light and began to rinse out some dishes while cradling the phone between her shoulder and ear.

"Well, I guess I'll let you go." His voice came through as warm and sensitive.

"I need to finish up a few things before I call it a night. I'll see you tomorrow, right?" She placed some items in the dish rack.

"Yeah. Sure."

The way he answered her left her a bit confused. Was he about to quit and pack up, once again hitting the road?

"Listen, Skip. You'd tell me if you weren't completely happy working for me, wouldn't you?"

"I don't see that being an issue," he said.

"What about staying in one place? Could that be an issue?"

"Maybe. But listen, I need to pay my tab and get back to the room. See you tomorrow."

SKIP HANDED the guy behind the bar a twenty-dollar bill. While he was making the change, Skip's mind wandered to their last words. Would he be able to tell her he wasn't happy? Would he be able to tell her Bozeman wasn't for him? The longer he stayed, the harder it would become. Tossing a couple of ones into the tip jar, he folded the remaining bills and secured the money into his pocket.

CHAPTER 10

Skip went from sitting in a dark corner of a drinking establishment to sitting in a dark corner of his room. Running his hand through his hair, he stopped suddenly, pounding the yellow leather chair arm with his fist. "What am I doing here?"

He began to pace the small room then slammed his body back into the chair, the cheap cushion flattening some. "She's making me be indecisive," he blurted to the four white walls.

The rapid thumping of the vein in his neck caused him to take notice. He placed two fingers on his pulse. "Get a grip, Skip." He practiced the breathing techniques he'd learned and closed his eyes. A loud growl came from his stomach. He'd forgotten to eat dinner. He grabbed his hat, sunglasses, and keys off the dresser and headed back out. Like a caged animal desiring to be set free, Skip had escaped.

Taking two steps at a time, he flew past the desk clerk to the outside. Breathing in the night air as soon as his shoes hit the pavement, Skip felt a calmness come over him. His long legs took him around the block and up the street. He had no idea where he was going, but the aroma of food led him to a place.

SO MUCH UNFINISHED business with that guy. What is he trying to tell me? Does he like me, does he want to get as far away from me as he can? Have I spooked him? Yeah, I probably have. Shelley's thoughts rambled endlessly through her mind.

"I have a commitment. I can't just run out and into his arms like some lovestruck teen. I have Billy to think of." She pulled her hair back into a pony and scrubbed her face red.

She blotted her face gently, dipping her finger into the eye cream. She dotted her lid, then under her eye, finally smoothing it out and around. She pumped night cream into her palm and slathered in on until it was barely sticky, then with the palm of her hand, pushed it into her skin, a trick an aesthetician taught her. Shuffling off to her bed, she slipped her slippers off and climbed under the covers. She knew she couldn't sleep. Not yet. He was too deep into her conscious for any slumber to come. Shelley plumped her pillow and pushed her back against it. Grabbing her novel off the nightstand, she turned to the page where the bookmark held her place and began reading.

Laying the book across her chest, she clasped her hands. This is why she didn't get involved. It never worked out. And especially with someone like Skip. He had too many issues for her. She couldn't bring him into her safe and secure nest with Billy. It just wouldn't work. Would it?

"I'll have a burger, medium rare. Hold the tomato and lettuce. Oh, and a beer. An amber ale if you have one on tap." He didn't even look at the menu. He ordered what he wanted and hoped for the best.

The waitress asked, "Fries or potato salad?"

"Fries. And bring me a side of mayo."

"You got it." She whirled around and headed to the kitchen to give the cook his order.

Skip looked around the lively joint. Several tables were occupied. Mostly tourists, he surmised. The glossy touristy magazines gave it away. He chuckled at his keen awareness and wondered if they'd ever been taken advantage of. He shook his head. People. Some could be so naïve.

"Here's your beer," she said, winking as she placed it on the table.

"Thanks."

"Sure. Can I get you anything else?" She didn't even try to cover up her flirty tone.

"No, that's it. Thanks."

She shrugged then danced away, swaying her hips, trying to get Skip's attention. He noticed. He didn't care. He could only think about Shelley and Billy.

After he chowed down on his burger and fries, he went for a long walk. All the streetlights were on and lit up the sidewalks nicely for those same naïve tourists who kept their wallets in their back pockets, and purses hanging off their shoulders for easy grabbing. He nodded and greeted the few he passed. Soon he was back to the B and B. Maybe now he could sleep? Yeah. Right.

"I MEAN, what does he want from me? I thought we had a connection. He almost kissed me. Twice." Shelley closed her book. It was no use. She kept reading the same paragraphs over and over. She set the book on the nightstand and tapped her head against the headboard. "Do I call him? Tell him how I feel? How *do* I feel?" She drew in her bottom lip.

A COLD SHOWER HELPED, but it wasn't until Skip put on his headphones to drown out any outside noise, and tuned into some easy listening tunes, he finally closed his eyes and somewhat rested. He never slept soundly anymore. Not since he went over there. But he was getting better, and the music helped. The one good piece of advice his new therapist gave him. Maybe the VA could help him after all. He'd had two sessions, and he liked the doctor. But he knew in order for him to help, Skip would have to be completely honest with him about a good many things.

"I KNOW. I'll say that I wanted to make sure he was coming to the shop tomorrow." Shelley let out a grunt. "That's just plain stupid, Shelley." She banged her head twice on the headboard. Her gaze traveled to her phone sitting next to the book. She reached for it and scrolled to his number, then she called him.

The phone rang and rang, finally going to his voice mail. Instead of leaving a message, she hung up.

"I knew it. That was a horrible idea." A tear bobbled on her bottom lid. Tossing the phone over to the table, she slid down, pulling the covers up to her chin and sobbed as quietly as she could.

SKIP WIDENED his eyes and sat straight up, his eyes adjusting to the dark. He pulled up the headphone on one ear, listening for sounds. He swore he heard something other than the music. He pulled off the rest of the equipment and got out of bed. His phone sat on the dresser, a blue light blinking. He'd missed a call. He strolled over and picked it up. "Shelley. She didn't leave a message."

He hit the redial button and waited.

THE RINGING of Shelley's phone snapped her out of her down-in-the-dumps mood. She almost dropped it, trying to answer it. "Hey. Is everything all right?" she asked.

"You called me."

"Oh, that's right. I did." A small giggle escaped her lips. "What did you have for dinner?"

"You called me to ask what I had for dinner? A burger and fries."

"We had leftovers."

"Leftover what?" he pressed.

"Spaghetti."

"Leftover spaghetti is pretty good. I always preferred it the next day. All the flavors meld together and it—"

"Skip. I called you because I need to know," she said, not letting him finish.

"Know what?"

"How you feel about me."

A long pause made her heart beat fast, and her throat constricted, making it difficult to swallow.

"I have to put all my cards on the table, Shelley. I care about you. And Billy. I'm very thankful for you giving me the job. I've told you that already. I enjoy spending time with you, but…I'm just not sure I can stay."

She gulped before she responded. She wondered if he could hear the noise. "Not sure you can stay? But I want you to. Billy wants you to."

"I know. This is why I never stay anywhere long, and it's absolutely why I don't get involved. I can't commit."

There was that word. She didn't have a choice in the matter when it came to Billy.

"I'll stick around until Damian is totally up to speed. Then I'm out of here."

He was so matter of fact that it angered her. How could he be so callous, so flippant about something as wonderful as a feeling of belonging. She'd never take that for granted. She knew what it felt like to get kicked to the curb. First by her family then by Billy's dad.

"Do what you want, Skip. There's no reason to hold someone back if they want to go. It's like trying to corral a wild horse or cage a zoo animal. You're free, Skip. I won't be the one to stand in your way."

"Shelley. I didn't mean to hurt you. I'm sorry."

"No. I'm sorry. I'm sorry for you. You'll never stay around long enough to form a lasting relationship. You'll never know how it feels to love someone, and they love you back."

"Shelley…"

"No, Skip. Don't. I'm good. I'm better than good. And after you're gone, I'll be better."

SKIP SLAMMED the phone down and yelled out in frustration. This conversation should have been saved for face to face, not over the airwaves. He didn't mean for it to all come out like it did, but sometimes, he had a difficult time holding back. Holding back never worked. In any situation.

"I KNEW IT. I put my heart out on my sleeve, and this is what I get." Shelley wiped the tears tumbling down her face. I will be fine. I will be fine, she repeated over and over. But would she? Probably not. And now tomorrow would be beyond awkward. "Men!"

HER FACE WAS in a large box as she pulled out packing paper to expose the contents. She kept her face hidden longer than necessary because she refused to make eye contact with him.

"Hey, Shelley," he said.

A muffled hello came from deep within the cardboard.

"We need to talk."

She could sense him being there. Close. The scent of his freshly laundered clothes wafted down into the dark space of the box. She slowly pulled her head out and rolled up, still trying to be angry, she glared at him.

"I think you said it all last night." She crossed her arms and rocked back on her heels.

"I can't help it. I feel like I can't breathe."

"If I'm doing that to you, then go. I would never want to be the cause of someone being not able to breathe," she said, mocking his choice of words.

"I'm not used to staying in one place," he added, trying to defend his position.

"I get it. You don't want to be here. Go. Go now. Don't wait any longer. The world beckons Skip Morrison," she said, seething mad and not hiding her sarcasm.

He placed his hand on her forearm.

She moved out of his touch.

"Shelley. Please," he said.

"Please? Seriously. You messed with our heads. Billy already misses having a father figure in his life. His grandfather doesn't even know him. And now, I have to tell him Skip is skipping out on us. No pun intended." She furrowed her brows.

"That's a cheap shot. You know better than to get mixed up with me. You can't tell me your single woman guard didn't fly up when I walked into this shop a month ago."

"Yes, it did. And that's why I'm only giving you part of the blame. I'll take the other for being a lame judge of character."

"I told you I was a drifter. I told you I had issues." He moved back away from her.

"You did." She turned back to her box.

"For what it's worth, I do care about you guys. I think you deserve better is all."

She reared up quickly, taking two giant steps toward him. With her hands balled, she pounded his chest. "You hurt me. You son of a—"

He grabbed her arms before she could wail another punch. She leaned into his chest and began to cry.

"Shelley," he murmured while caressing her. "It was the furthest thing from my mind."

CHAPTER 11

Shelley and Billy didn't see Skip again after that. As far as she knew, he drove off with the same few belongings he came with, and except for the truck, he was traveling light. She tried to not think about him, but he'd left such a hole in her heart. Billy asked about him for the first couple of weeks, but after that, just like giving up on his father, he gave up on Skip. Lately, Shelley thought about her own father. A vivid image of their house, the one she grew up in, came into her mind. She could see all the rooms and furnishings and wondered if it was still the same. She wondered if they even thought about her. Or Billy.

She toyed with calling them, but what would she say? Hey, this is your daughter, the one you turned your back on?

As summer waned to an end, the temperatures also cooled down. Fall festivities were all abuzz in the town, and like most residents of Bozeman, fall was a time for rejoicing and rejuvenating. She and Billy stopped by the nightly market to pick up some produce. It was a great way to rub elbows with the townspeople. She ran into several customers, but her eyes lit up when she saw Jennie with her three kids in tow.

"Jennie!" She wrapped her arms around her and pulled her in for a hug.

"Shelley. Billy." She stepped back and smiled. "You remember my kiddos. This is Lacey, Jeremy, and Josh." She moved her hand to each head as she called their names.

"It's so nice to see you guys. This is my son Billy." Shelley gently put her hand behind his back, encouraging him to step forward.

"You're getting so big," Jennie said, smiling ear to ear.

"Do you guys want to grab a bite to eat? I hear the corn-dogs are to die for," Shelley asked.

"You read our mind. We were headed over there," Jennie said.

The six of them meandered toward the corndog booth. Shelley ordered the food and insisted on paying the tab. But when she had to hear over a dozen times, "thank you, and you shouldn't have," she suggested Jennie pay it forward sometime. That seemed to satisfy her, and she then graciously accepted Shelley's kindness.

"I will. In fact, I'm going to be thinking about it all night how I can do that," Jennie said as she munched on her corndog.

After they finished eating, Shelley offered the next hand of kindness. "Let us give you a ride home."

"You don't have to do that. The bus is going to come in twenty minutes."

"Please let us drop you off."

"Okay. If you insist. It will be nice to get home sooner."

"Good. Then it's settled. Let's go."

Jennie's house was modest, but the grounds were well kept. The white picket fence around the property and the mums bursting in yellow and orange showed she cared for her home. The only thing missing from the driveway was a car.

"How are you doing with that down payment?" Shelley turned to Jennie, and a quietness came over them.

"If there's anything I can do to help." Skip flashed into her mind. He was supposed to help with this. "I would like to help."

"That's very thoughtful of you. I'm trying to figure a few things out. Right now, the property taxes are due on the house. My main goal is to make sure we have a roof over our head and food in the pantry. The rest has to wait."

Shelley watched as Jennie and her children exited the car and walked up to the stoop. She turned and waved, then gave each kid a nudge to do the same.

"Thank you, Ms. Bennett, for the ride," Lacey, the eldest called out.

"I like those kids," Billy said, kicking the seat back and humming a tune.

"They are very nice," Shelley agreed.

After tucking Billy into bed, Shelley did one of the hardest things she'd ever done. Well, the second hardest thing. She called her parents.

"Who is this?" a gruff voice said.

"It's me. Shelley."

"Shelley?"

"Yes, Dad. It's me. How are you?"

He grumbled a second then cleared his throat. "Cora, come quick. It's Shelley"

"Hello?" a meek and mild voice said.

"Mom? It's nice to hear your voice."

"Where are you?"

"Montana."

"Montana? Have you been there all along?"

"I love it here. Billy and I are in Bozeman."

"Billy." Her mom's voice dropped off.

"He's five going on fourteen. He has a birthday next month."

"My my," her mother said.

"Listen, I know it's been a long time, and we certainly can't patch things up overnight, but Billy and I are missing you. We need you all in our life. Can't you just put aside your beliefs and let's move forward. For the sake of one of the sweetest little boys you'll ever know?"

Shelley was proud of herself. It took a lot of courage to put all her cards on the table. If she could get her mother to see the light, maybe she'd be able to convince Henry, Shelley's father.

"I think we can do that. Henry and I have been thinking about you both. We didn't know how to find you."

They weren't internet savvy, and Shelley wasn't even sure they had cell phones.

"So, Daddy wants to see us too?"

"Why don't you come home and we'll sort it all out?"

"I had another idea. The holidays are coming. Why don't you guys come out here? Bozeman is so pretty in the winter. We have a lot of festivities coming up over the next couple of months. Billy is excited about dressing up for Halloween, then we have Thanksgiving followed by Christmas. We'd love for you to visit anytime." Shelley spoke fast, getting all her words out before she changed her mind.

"Okay. Let me discuss it with your father. What's a good number to call you at?"

CHAPTER 12

Staring out the window, Shelley gazed steadily at the trees. The leaves were turning shades of yellow and orange, a telltale sign fall was upon them. She needed a brief distraction from the phone call she'd just had with her mother. It went surprisingly well. Maybe enough time had passed that they'd forgiven her. Forgiven her? For what? For falling in love and having a child. "I hope they don't play that card," she said out loud. "I have nothing to be forgiven for," she mused.

THE HOLIDAYS always meant shopping and who didn't like to receive gifts? Shelley decorated the shop with orange, brown, and yellow and created some window displays to entice shoppers to come inside and take a look. She'd just unpacked some new items she was particularly pleased with, hoping they'd go over well with the townspeople of Bozeman, and any lurking tourists this late in the season. There were always those folks who loved snowcapped mountains, cups of freshly brewed coffee and pastries while enjoying the cold weather. Shelley was on the fence about the winter weather in Bozeman. She'd often thought she was more of a southern California girl where the temperatures rarely fluctuated from seventy-six degrees. But alas that would not come to fruition. Bozeman called to her and now was their home. She put the finishing touches on her display and stood back to admire it. Crystal pumpkins and gourds in various hues of orange, gold, and green sitting on top of apple crates with silk leaves of varying same colors gently and creatively scattered around made her smile. Her concentration broke when the phone in her shop rang. She scooted across the store to grab it.

"Hello?"

"Hey," a man's voice said.

She immediately recognized it as the voice of Skip. She began to walk around with the phone, giving her some time before she said anything else.

"Are you there?"

"Yes. Yes, I'm here." She straightened a shelf, lining up merchandise to the edge and moved to the next row.

"I've been thinking about you guys. How are you getting along?"

She erected her back straight as a board and pulled the phone away from her ear and looked at it strangely. "Really?" she whispered before placing the phone to her ear again.

"We're doing okay. Getting ready for the holiday shoppers. I just finished a display."

"For the window?"

"Pumpkins and gourds, and leaves…" she said, not sure why she was telling him.

"Good. Glad to hear you all are doing fine. I'm doing good too."

She didn't think to ask him. Why would she even care?

"Where did you end up at?" She couldn't help herself. She wanted to know.

"I'm in Cheyenne."

"Wyoming?"

"Yes. It's a lot like Montana."

"I guess so."

Their small talk left her feeling exhausted. Playing nice in the sandbox was hard. "Well, I'm glad you're doing okay."

"I think you already said that. Anyway, I wanted to know if I could come visit."

That statement totally blindsided her. She didn't see it coming, and it was broad daylight. "Come here? To see us?" She walked to the end of the shop, whirled around, and walked back toward the counter.

"I'd like to see Billy."

"Billy?"

"And you. I'd like to see you."

"Skip. I can't have you just bouncing in and out of our lives. That's not fair to us. We've moved on." She didn't want to let him know she thought about him nearly every night, and she'd caught Billy during his nighttime prayers asking for him to come back.

"I understand. But it would mean a lot to me. And besides, I totally forgot we were going to help Jennie out with a fund-raiser to get her the cash for her car."

"Yeah. You sure did. I haven't even done anything. I don't know where to begin."

"Let me help. I'll be in Bozeman the end of next week."

"Okay," she said, defeated.

"Shelley?"

"Yes?"

"It was great to hear your voice."

She hung up the phone in a daze. This couldn't be happening. Not now.

HER BRAIN FOG made it hard to concentrate once again. The phone conversation she'd had with her mom followed by Skip left her feeling a bit confused. Too many things were happening all at once. She'd tried to put her feelings in check and move forward, and she thought she'd done a pretty good job. And then just like the couple standing on the sidelines of the dance floor waiting for their cue of music, those feelings came waltzing back in. She shuddered. Could she go through any more heartache?

Thank goodness she had Rock Paper Scissors to keep her busy. With the daily delivery of new items and the influx of shoppers, she barely thought about Skip's visit. Her parents, on the other hand, she couldn't stop thinking about. She'd pick up a crystal figurine, and it would bring back memories of her mother's china cabinet where she displayed trinkets. She stacked boxes of stationery, and when she placed the one with daffodils, it reminded her of her mother's flower garden. And when she went to rearrange the display of colored pencils and other craft supplies on a table in the far corner of the shop, she remembered the time she and her dad made a structure out of popsicle sticks.

At the end of the week, she was ready to put her feet up and relax.

When Shelley picked up Billy from school, she made a conscious decision not to tell him about Skip's visit. For one, she wasn't even one hundred percent sure he'd follow through, and there was no way she'd disappoint her little boy. She'd not even told him about his grandparent's upcoming visit. Nothing was set in stone, and hurting his feelings was the last thing on her mind.

"Did you have a good day?"

"Yes! We went on a field trip to the children's museum. I made this." He held up a piece of painted wood.

"It's so pretty. What is it?" She studied the four-by-four-inch square.

"It's just something I made." He puffed out his little chest and offered up a cheesy grin.

"Well, you did a great job. I'll cherish it forever." She wrapped her arm around her son and led him to the car.

"What are we going to have for dinner?" he asked.

She'd not really planned anything. And it was during these nights when she didn't have the energy or desire to prepare a meal, and they were tired of fast food that she'd come up with a night of snacking. Healthy snacks. She'd cut up slices of fruit and vegetables, put out some crackers, cheese, and deli ham, and they'd make little sandwiches. She'd have a glass of red wine to wash it all down with, and he'd have a juice box. And if they were still hungry after all that, she'd offer him a bowl of ice cream. She figured the dinner contained all the essential elements of a good dinner, and he had fun thinking he was snacking instead of having dinner. It worked for them.

"Mommy?" he asked as he grabbed a cheese cube.

"Yes, dear." She drew the wineglass to her mouth and sipped.

"I love you."

"I love you too."

"Today at school, the kids were talking about their grandparents visiting for Christmas. Why don't I have any?"

Shelley studied her son's face. The look of true innocence flashed in his eyes. She swallowed hard before answering him. "You do. They just live far away."

She should have known that would not satisfy her intelligent child.

"They could take a plane. That's what Peter's grandparents are going to do."

She pursed her lips tightly.

"I would like for my grandparents to come visit me. Can you call them and tell them that?"

A tear tried to force entry onto her bottom lid. She willed it away, but then soon after another came then another.

"Mommy, why are you crying?"

His sad face brightened hers, and soon she let out a small giggle. "I will, Billy. I'll call them for you. I'll let them know of your request." She brushed the tears away and held out her arms.

"Thank you!" He jumped up, flinging himself into her embrace, his arms wrapping around her neck, as he began to peck kisses on her cheek.

She lowered her hands and tickled his sides. He started laughing so hard he jumped off her lap and ran down the hall, yelling, "I gotta pee."

Shelley slumped into her chair. *That kid. He keeps me grounded.*

It came to her while leaning in to tuck him in for the night. He had a familiar look all of a sudden, and it wasn't from his father. It was from her father. The shape of his mouth and eyes reminded Shelley of Henry.

"Good night, Billy," she whispered as she closed the door, leaving it ajar.

The thumping in her chest as she dialed their number was enough to make her hang up. But when she heard his voice, she closed her eyes and spoke.

"Hi, Daddy. It's me."

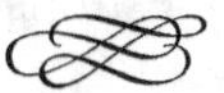

CHAPTER 13

"Hi, Shelley. It's nice to hear from you again."

His tone was soft and inviting, and it brought tears to her eyes. She'd missed them. Missed them being a part of their lives.

"I was wondering if you all decided about my request for a visit?"

"Mother was going to call you tomorrow, but you beat her to it. We got the plane tickets. We'll be there Wednesday."

"This Wednesday?" She tried to level the shock in her response.

"That's all right, isn't it?"

"Yes, of course. I didn't know you'd all come out that fast. Billy is really looking forward to meeting you. He's been talking a lot about his grandparents. The other kids…well, they have been talking to him about theirs, and he's got a bunch of questions is all."

"We are dying to meet him as well. Too much time has passed. We need to move on, forgive and forget."

"I've forgiven you, Daddy. You and Mom both. I want you in our lives."

"Forgive us? What did we do? If I remember correctly it was you that disappointed us."

Silence came over her. Could she possibly be hearing what she thought she heard?

"You're kidding, right? That's not even funny, though. You guys turned your back on us. I recall exactly what happened."

"You chose him over us. That's what happened," Henry bellowed.

"Chose my child over you? I sure did. And I'd do it again every time that same scenario presented itself. We don't have anything else to discuss. I hope you can get your money back for the tickets."

"Shelley. Don't. That's not what I mean. Think of your mother." Henry stopped quickly.

"I can't, Daddy. If you guys feel I have something to apologize for, you're sadly mistaken. Take care."

Shelley cupped her face and cried into her hands. This didn't go the way she'd hoped it would. And now she'd have to tell Billy that his grandparents were never coming.

WITH SWOLLEN EYES, Shelley opened the shop and tried to be cheerful with every customer that came in. When they asked her what happened, she'd reply, "allergies?" It seemed to ward off additional questioning. When she could, she'd go into the bathroom and splash cold water on her face. It didn't really help. Only time would reduce the inflammation. But with a heavy heart, she mustered through the rest of the day, trying to force a smile and behave as if she were the happiest of people.

She stayed open a few minutes past her regular closing time to help an elderly gentleman pick out a gift for his great-niece. He was a jolly fellow and quite a character, cracking jokes here and there, bringing a wide grin to her face and laughter. He was just what she needed to round out her miserable day.

Billy was his jovial self. Running through the house with his Batman cape on, knocking down Lego pieces and jumping from the couch to the chair.

"Whoa, mister. What do you think you're doing?" Shelley halted him by grabbing his shirt sleeve.

"I'm Batman. I'm jumping from the high buildings."

"That's Superman who does that," Shelley said, correcting him.

"No, Mom. Batman does it too." He folded his legs and bounced on the cushion.

"Furniture is for what?" she asked.

"Sitting," he said with a scowl.

"Dinner will be ready in five minutes. Go wash up."

Over fried bologna and cheese sandwiches on English muffins and chicken noodle soup, Billy engaged in conversation with Shelley about his day. She tried to tell him about the older man who came in, but it just reminded her of grandparents and decided to forgo the details.

She wanted to tell Billy about Skip calling and the plans of his visit, but she felt he was too fragile to commit, and she didn't trust he wouldn't flake out on them. Disappointing Billy was the last thing she'd do.

Sitting alone in her living room, feeling deflated and defeated, she began to feel sorry for herself. She was a good person, right? She tried to help those less fortunate. She did everything she could to make a nice home for Billy. She held a steady job, provided food and a roof over their heads. Why then did everything feel so lonely and dreary?

She took a few deep breaths and then called. This time the only courage she had was contained well within her.

"I was just thinking about you," he said.

"Oh?"

"I'm sitting here devising a plan to help Jennie."

"Really?"

"Yes. I know Halloween is big in Bozeman. Why don't we have an open house at your shop? We'll advertise for the children to come in costume to the store, get candy, and in return, give a small donation to help Jennie. But we won't say it's for Jennie. We'll just say it's for a

Bozeman resident. That way if she comes with her kids, she won't know what we're up to."

"I love that idea, Skip. You've put some thought into it."

"I want to help. It's called paying it forward."

She crossed her legs at the ankle and rested her shoulders back into the deep cushions of the couch. She liked the way he thought.

"Let's add one more thing into this. In return for the donation, we can provide pictures. I can get someone to take them. I have a cute scarecrow display complete with a bale of hay in the corner of the store. It would be a perfect setting for photos. That way, they'll feel like they are getting something in return for the donation."

"Who are you going to get to do the photos?"

"I know this guy at the high school who teaches photography. I know he'd be happy to help."

"What is it with you and the teaching staff at the high school?" He laughed.

"I met him through Quincy. I know a lot of people here. It doesn't mean anything." Her tone was defensive, but she didn't care.

"Hey, no worries. I was just curious. I'm not insinuating anything."

She cleared her throat before continuing. "I loved Billy's dad. I wanted nothing more than to be his wife and the mother of his child. I gave up my family for him."

"I know. And I also think it's time to rekindle your relationship with them."

She didn't have the heart or the energy to tell him what had transpired over the last couple of days. It was too raw to discuss without her choking up.

"We can talk about it when you come."

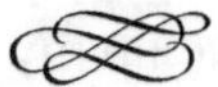

CHAPTER 14

Shelley tried to keep her heart from jumping out of her chest, but the anxiety of seeing him again came busting through. Her clammy palms, the little trickle of sweat beads above her brow along with the tightening of her stomach, told her she was one hot mess.

In keeping with the theme of Halloween, Shelley dressed as a witch. Her long black fingernails kept getting caught on things, and her pointed hat would abruptly fall off or flop into her eyes when she least expected it. Tired of combating both the nails and the hat, she retired them to the back room. If she didn't bite her nails, a nervous habit she was unable to break, she could have opted for nail color. Oh well. The show must go on, she thought.

No sign of Skip made her even more anxious. She was so glad she didn't tell Billy. He would have been so disappointed. She wondered where Skip had run to now.

The corner was set up for the pictures. Along a long table draped in purple and black sat a huge rubber pumpkin filled to the top with candy, on the other side a large clear container with an orange ribbon tied around it for donations. Shelley had invited the community by word of mouth and a small ad in the Bozeman Weekly, a free publication residents could pick up at any of the town merchants. She nervously looked at her watch. The line of people was forming. Soon, she'd open the doors for the first annual Shop, Trick, or Treat. If it became a success, she'd consider having it every year, sponsoring another worthwhile cause.

She walked over to the door and turned the deadbolt and opened the door wide. "Welcome, everyone."

In walked the first family. A mom and dad with their two children. After that a dad and his son. When she made eye contact with the next person, she almost asked him if he was a little old for trick or treat, but when he smiled, despite his face cloaked in a hooded shirt, she knew instantly it was Skip dressed up.

Sizing him up, she said, "Let's see. I know that costume

from somewhere." She thumped her mouth as she thought.

"Robin Hood," he said, beaming with pride.

"Ah yes. Robin Hood. I didn't expect to see you, in costume or not."

"I told you I would." He dipped down and gave her a small peck on the cheek.

Startled by his gesture, she stepped back.

"I'm sorry. I was just happy to see you." He took her arm, and they moved out of the way of the crowd.

"I thought you might come earlier. Not as I opened the doors." Now her tone showed a bit of irritation.

"I had a flat tire, or I would have been here earlier."

"The old flat tire trick, huh?" She raised her brows and smirked.

"I really did. Anyway," he said, looking over the top of her as he watched the line form over by the scarecrow. "The town came out to show their support, didn't they?"

She nodded. "I'm very happy to see so many."

"Where's Billy?" He looked around, then met her eyes again.

"He's over by the display."

He began to walk over near all the people. She followed behind. Billy looked up right at the moment they were approaching, and when he saw Skip, he pushed his way through the crowd, yelling his name. Shelley didn't want to admit it, but it made her feel so giddy inside.

Billy leaped into Skip's arms. "Skip. You're here!"

"Happy Halloween," Skip sang out.

"Do you want some candy? We have a bunch over there," he said, motioning behind him.

"Maybe later. I need to talk to your mom. You have fun." He lowered him to the floor.

Billy rushed back to his post at the table.

"Can we talk in private?" His eyes never wavered from her.

Swallowing down the growing lump in her throat, she slowly nodded. "In the back?"

Her long skirt swooshed down the hall along with the clicking of their heels. She stepped inside the workroom first. She whirled around to find him inches from her. She gulped.

"I missed you. I should have never run off like that. Can you forgive me?" He moved in closer, sliding his hands around her waist.

"There's nothing to forgive you for, Skip. You made your decision. I'd never hold you back. If you need wide-open spaces, then that's what I'll give you. I just can't have you coming back into our lives and then leaving like some swinging door."

"I don't want that either. I've been talking to a shrink. She's really helping me. I want to come back. Come back to you and Billy." He pulled her in.

She tried to resist, but it was no use. He was like a magnet drawing her in. Reaching up, she traced the line of a muscle up his arm. She could feel her chest rise and fall in anticipation of the kiss. The kiss they never seemed to finish.

Leaning in for the kiss, Skip stopped millimeters from her mouth. A small breathless whisper escaped her lips. "Kiss me," she said.

She clung to his broad shoulders as he ran his hand behind her, settling on her neck. He deepened the kiss, taking her breath away and making her knees feel wobbly. When he broke off the kiss, while still holding her, he looked deep into her eyes, causing her to squirm in his arms. It was scary how much she felt at this moment.

"Finally. No interruptions." He swayed her gently in his strong arms.

"Skip, please don't hurt us. I don't think I could handle that."

"I won't. I'm moving back. I have my duffel bag in the truck. I made reservations at the B and B, and I have my first appointment at the VA tomorrow."

Her gaze darted from his mouth to his eyes and back to his mouth. Raising up on her toes, she reached for him, pulling him in for another kiss.

AFTER THE LAST family exited the shop, Shelley locked up behind them. It'd been an exhausting but fun-filled evening. She studied the face of her watch, calculating how much time she had before she had to get Billy to bed. Maybe all he'd have time for tonight was a spit bath.

"Let's count the money," Billy chanted over and over.

Rolling back on her heels, she hugged her arms. "Okay, but then we have to go. You need to get in bed soon." She looked down at him with loving eyes.

Skip dumped the container on the table and began separating the bills and putting the coins in piles. Shelley brought out the paper coin rolls and started collecting them. When they finished counting, and the number was said out loud, she couldn't believe her ears. "How much?"

"Fifteen hundred and eleven dollars and fifty cents," he said.

"That will make a nice down payment on a car, won't it?"

"It will after I add my contribution," Skip said, gathering up the money and placing it in a small cloth sack.

"I haven't added mine yet, either." She dug inside her purse, pulling out two twenties.

"I have to give you mine tomorrow. I didn't have any pockets." He lowered his eyes to his skin-tight black leggings.

She raised her brows up and down. He was pretty sexy in that outfit. "No problem. I have to get Billy home. School tomorrow, and we're really behind schedule."

He walked them out, ensuring they got into their car safely. Bozeman was a pretty safe town, but she knew he'd seen too many bad things in his life. He ducked into the open car window and reached his arm inside, touching her arm. "Good night. I'll see you tomorrow."

The sweet smell of his warm breath wafted below her nose. "Sure." She started the engine.

"I do have my old job back, right?" He stepped back as she popped the transmission into reverse.

"I don't know. You'll have to ask Damian."

"What?"

"I made him supervisor of engraving. You'll have to ask him if you can come back."

She drove off smiling, and when she peered into the rearview mirror, he was smiling too.

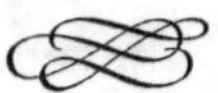

CHAPTER 15

*D*riving home had a totally different feeling than other times. Shelley hummed softly as she turned the steering wheel onto the road. Billy's droopy eyelids and yawns let her know any chance of a real bath would not be happening.

"Thank you for being a big boy tonight and helping me. I really appreciate that." She waited for his response before continuing.

"Uh-huh. You're welcome."

"Are you tired?"

"Yes."

"I tell you what. Just brush your teeth and hop into bed when we get home. I'll spray you down tomorrow."

He laughed at that. "Spray me down with the hose?" He giggled again.

"Yeah. In the backyard."

He grabbed his tummy and roared with laughter.

Finally, something to laugh about. Shelley grinned. *Skip Morrison, I swear. You better be true to us.*

SHELLEY RUSHED TO THE SHOP, hoping to see Damian first. She paced the store, waiting for him. When she finally saw him bop inside, wearing his earplugs, no doubt listening to music, she waved at him to get his attention. He pulled out the earplugs. She could hear the music.

"You know, you could damage your hearing by listening to loud music so close to your eardrums."

He furrowed his brows as he listened.

"But that's not what I wanted to tell you. Skip is back in town."

"Awesome. I sure could use the help."

"Let's don't make it too easy on him."

"Beg for his old job back? Why?"

"To let him know he can't leave us hanging like that again."

"Us? You mean you and Billy, don't you?"

Damian was years beyond his age of nineteen. She tipped her chin. "Yes. He hurt us. I don't want him to leave again." Why she felt compelled to let him in on her hurt even surprised her.

"I'll let him plead a bit, but man, I can't dis my mentor like that. He's taught me so much, and has helped me in more ways than I can ever repay him."

She knew he'd helped Damian out with a few nights at the B and B, but what else had he done?

"How so?"

"He paid for an entire month over at the B and B and helped me with a down payment for my car."

"He did all that for you? I had no idea."

"Yeah. He's a great guy. I just can't be too hard on him, ya know?"

"Okay. Never mind then. When he comes in, welcome him back with open arms. I can only hope he stays around."

"Thanks, Shelley."

Damian shuffled his feet down the hall toward the work area. Soon after, Skip made his entrance.

"Good morning. Isn't it a beautiful day?" His wide grin showed off his perfect teeth.

"Yes, it is. Damian is waiting for you."

"I hope he takes me back. I need the job." He winked as he moved down the hall.

He knew full well Damian would take him back. He was teasing her. She burst into a wide smile, thankful her back was to him so he couldn't see.

Damian must have put Skip right to work. He didn't come out of the back room until after lunchtime.

"I'm starving. Can I bring you back anything for lunch?" he asked.

"I brought mine. But thank you." She lowered her eyes back to the document she'd been reading.

"We have to talk about last night at some point."

She slowly rolled her head upward and locked eyes with him.

"The kiss. The moment. How it made us feel," he said boldly.

She nervously looked around to make sure no one was in earshot. "It made me feel good inside. Warm and cozy like a cup of hot chocolate on a cold winter day. You know, with a dollop of whipped cream and a cherry on top." She modeled a sly smile.

"That's a pretty spectacular kiss then." He moved to the counter and rested his hands on the display case.

She slid her hands out and touched the tips of his fingers. "I'd say so."

"I need a repeat. Just to make sure it was worthy of the dollop of whipped cream and the cherry on top." He pulled her hands into his and squeezed them.

Her quickened pulse shot through her body, and the radiant feeling spread like wildfires on a hot day in a dry forest. "Okay." A whisper squeaked out.

"Tonight." He raised her hands and kissed them.

"Skip. Not here," she pleaded, not sure how far he was going to go.

He quickly let her hands drop and shot backward. Whirling around, he said, "I'm off to get lunch. I'll be back soon."

She pressed her fingers to her lips, tasting his touch. She was falling for him. Falling for him hard.

The day flew by for Shelley, and before she realized, it was closing time. Damian and Skip came out of the back room, laughing loudly.

"What's so funny?" she asked.

"Skip was telling me about his flat tire."

Shelley cast her gaze toward Skip. He pursed his lips and nodded.

"The flat tire that made me late. You know. The one you didn't believe happened."

"Whatever, Skip," she said, not amused.

"He went to take the tire off, and it started rolling down the hill. He ran to grab it, and the jack fell, messing up his rim. He had one thing after another happen to him." Damian slapped Skip on the back. "But a pretty little lady came to the rescue and made it all better."

Shelley widened her eyes. "Pretty lady? You left that part out." She turned around, determined not to give him the satisfaction of making her sweat.

"It wasn't like that. She stopped and asked if she could help. I told her no, and she went on her merry way."

Damian snickered.

Shelley stood in front of the cash register. "As I said, Skip Morrison. Who cares?" She hit the button, and the cash drawer flew open. She began to count the bills, putting them in the bank bag.

"See you tomorrow, Skip," Damian said.

Shelley leaned over and gripped the pencil. She began to enter amounts onto the ledger. Skip left a huge roll of bills held by a rubber band in front of her.

"What's this?"

"My donation toward Jennie's car."

Shelley snapped the band off and began to flip through the one-hundred-dollar bills. When she finished counting, she looked up. "Skip, there is over eight thousand dollars here."

"I know. Eight thousand, four hundred, and forty-eight to be exact."

She tipped her head and stared upward, counting to herself. When she lowered her eyes, she met his. "That means we have ten thousand dollars to give her."

He dug into his pocket and flipped a fifty-cent piece on the counter. It rolled on its side then wobbled over. "Now we do."

Shelley laughed. "Right to the penny."

"When are we going to present it to her?"

"I was going to do it soon. But you know what…I'm wondering if we could just buy her a car outright. Ten thousand dollars is nothing to sneeze at."

"True, but cars are expensive. But maybe we could get one of the dealers to give us a really good deal based on Jennie's plight. They could write off the rest and call it their portion of the donation," Skip said.

"Are you free tonight?" Shelley gathered the rest of the bills and change from the register and tossed them into the green money bag.

"Sure."

"Let's go pick up Billy and head out to Tom Flannigan's Auto Mart."

"Burgers and shakes for dinner?" He winked.

"Billy would love that."

CHAPTER 16

Shelley and Skip shook hands with Tom, sealing the deal on a shiny red SUV with low mileage. It happened so fast it turned both of their heads. Once they sat down with him and explained what they were trying to do, he was all on board. He told them he was trying to find a nice thing to do during the holiday season and this idea of giving a car to a family in need fit the bill. They worked out all the details of delivery, and when Shelley and Skip were satisfied, they exited the dealership with Billy in the middle, Shelley on one side, Skip on the other, holding hands and singing, burgers and shakes over and over.

Billy had scarfed down his burger because he wanted to go off and play. He saw some kids he knew climbing on the indoor playground equipment and was biting at the bit to join them.

"Go ahead. But stay where I can see you," Shelley said, leveling a warning.

Shelley dipped her french fry in mayonnaise and popped it into her mouth.

Skip nodded toward the creamy condiment. "Not everyone likes mayo with their fries."

"I've always done it. I'm not a big ketchup fan. The mayonnaise brings out the flavor of the potato."

"I know. I learned that little trick when I stopped over in Germany," Skip said, dipping his fries in her mayo.

"I'm so happy about the car for Jennie and her children, aren't you?" she said.

"I am. I think it's a wonderful opportunity to give back. You're so thoughtful." He touched her hand, sending shivers down her spine.

"I'm going to take that money to the bank and get a money order made out to her. We'll tie a big red bow around the car and present her with the check. It will go for car insurance and gas."

"Don't forget car seats. She'll need at least one for her youngest," Skip said.

Shelley softened her face. He really was attentive. He knew about children and car seats. What a guy. She nodded. "True. And this money will help her get that."

"Can we talk about us now?" Skip turned toward the play structure. Billy was still jumping around and playing with his friends.

Shelley drew in a deep breath and let it out. "Sure. We're alone."

"I want to let you know how important you guys are to me. I never once stopped thinking about you."

"Okay."

"You believe me, don't you?" He spoke softly.

"I guess I do. I'm just not sure why you left."

"I told you. I was feeling scared. I'm not used to staying in one place."

"What will make it different for you this time? It's still the same place, we're the same people." She drew back and sat deep into the molded chair, feeling the wood against her back.

"I'm getting help for my anxiety. I'm working through it. Slowly but surely as my shrink says." He chuckled, then picked up his drink and held it.

"I'm glad you're getting help. I had encouraged you to do that before—" She held back from finishing her sentence.

"Before I jumped in my truck and ran away," he said, finishing it for her.

"Something like that."

"Mommy, look at me."

Both of them turned their heads. Billy was at the top of the slide.

"Be careful," Shelley called out before moving her attention back to Skip.

"I rented an apartment."

"You did?"

"I told you. I'm serious about sticking around." He put his drink down and reached for her hands.

"Skip, Billy and I have been through so much. I want you to stay, but only if that's what you want. See, the way I feel about it is this. You can't corral a wild horse. It will eventually jump the fence. Do you understand the analogy I'm trying to make?"

"Yes. But, every now and then you come across a mustang that wants to be tamed."

Her breath quickened, and her rapid pulse plummeted through her veins. She squeezed his hands but said nothing.

Billy came rushing over to the table and broke the moment. Shelley was happy he did. They'd both said what was on their mind. It was time for them to prove it to each other. He dropped them off at the house. He'd promised Billy during the drive back he'd come in for a second. Billy wanted to show him something. While the two were in Billy's bedroom, laughing and talking loudly about boy stuff, Shelley's phone rang. She let it go to voice mail. They weren't going to destroy one of the happiest evenings she'd had in a long time.

"I'm off. See you tomorrow," Skip said, snuggling up close to her.

Shelley looked toward Billy's bedroom. She didn't want him to see them kissing. It would only confuse him.

After his mouth met hers, she stepped back. "Good night."

He reared his head back and studied her.

"What?"

"That was a little kiss. After today, I thought I would get a little more."

"You thought wrong. I have Billy to consider."

"Okay," he said, rocking back on his heels and moving backward. "I get it. I won't push. When you're ready, I'm here." He blew her a kiss and turned toward the door.

"Skip."

He halted, whirling around. "Already?" He laughed as he moved toward her.

She flattened her hands on his chest to stop him from getting closer. "No, not that."

He lowered his hands to her waist and held her. "Then what?"

"My parents. I thought we were getting somewhere, then my dad went and said something stupid and messed everything up. Having grandparents is so important to Billy. He's hurting inside. First, his dad abandons him, and then his grandparents." A tear trickled down her cheek.

"What did your dad say?"

"He tried to say I owe them an apology. Then he said he forgave me. And I have nothing to be forgiven for. It was them who turned their back on us."

"Okay, slow down. What exactly transpired those years ago?"

"I got pregnant. I wanted to keep my baby. My only mistake was the man who I chose. He was a jerk. My parents were right about him, but I can't turn the hands of time back."

"True. They were probably more scared than anything. Parents, especially dads, have a propensity to say dumb things sometimes. Was that who was calling you?" He nodded toward her phone on the counter.

"Yes. I didn't want a big argument."

"Choose your words carefully. Maybe write them down. After Billy is asleep call them back. I can stay if you want." He rocked her in his arms.

"You'd do that for me?"

"I told you. I'm here for you both." He leaned in and kissed her.

She welcomed his warm lips by kissing him back. "Give me a few minutes to get Billy settled in for the night. Why don't you sit down and make yourself comfortable?"

She did the quickest tuck-in job on Billy ever. She read two paragraphs, kissed him on the cheek, and turned off the lights. As she began to close the door, he spoke in a tired, small voice.

"Tell Skip good night for me."

"I will."

"I took the liberty of jotting a few things down. But you don't have to use any of them. It might just be a starting place with your folks." He shoved the tablet toward her.

She scanned the items. "These are good. I like that one. Uh-huh. Okay." She held the table out. "These are wonderful, Skip. How'd you know?"

"I had to do a similar exercise regarding the ex-wife. It was to help get my aggression out."

"Did it work?"

"I think so. I'm here, aren't I?"

"You mean, you did this recently?"

"The doc suggested I call her and tell her how I felt about things but also to let her know I forgave her. I'm not saying you have anything to be forgiven for, but that's how I approached it."

"Was she receptive?"

"She'd had a lot of time to think about what she did. Turns out the guy she left me for dumped her. Her life is more of a mess than mine if you can believe that. Anyway, we are putting everything behind us. I wished her well, she wished me likewise. Once I did that, I could move on a bit. At least with relationships and women. I still have to overcome my reaction to loud and eruptive noises, and my fear of four walls closing in, but I've made such progress."

"I think you have. You have a great job, a wonderful boss," she said, patting herself on the shoulder. "And now an apartment."

"Yep. And I have you and Billy. As long as I have you two by my side, I can get through everything else." He stroked the cushion next to him. "Sit. Let's call your parents."

She reluctantly moved to the couch and sat. She wasn't sure she was ready for this big step. Calling her parents with her… err boyfriend. Boyfriend. Skip Morrison was her boyfriend. A big smile wrapped around her face. I have a boyfriend, she thought.

She picked up the phone and called. When her mom answered, her heart leaped. "Mom. This is Shelley."

"I'm so happy you called. I think there's been a big misunderstanding," her mom said.

"I want to move forward, Mom. We can't live in the past." She read from the notes. "I don't want to rehash stuff. But I do think it's important for all of us to get our hurt feelings out in the open once and for all, then not talk about it anymore. So, I'll start. I love you guys. I want you in my life. Billy craves having family. I made a mistake. But only one. That was when I left home and moved in with Billy's dad. But it's not a mistake worth tearing our family apart any longer. I love my son. He's the reason I get up each and every day."

"I know, dear. A child is a precious being. You did the right thing. It's just hard for your dad with you being the only girl and child. He loves you. That's all."

"I need Dad to tell me that."

"Henry. Come to the phone."

Shelley covered the mouthpiece. "She's getting him," she whispered.

Skip nodded for encouragement, then mouthed to her, *you can do it.*

"Hello," a no-nonsense voice said.

"Dad. Let's start over."

"How are we to do that?"

"I am not going to apologize for having Billy. I'm not going to express regret for trying to be a family with the man I thought I loved. I'll only say that I am sorry it didn't work out the way I had thought it would. But turning your back on us was an awful thing to do. I believe you owe me an apology."

The pause between the cell lines was long and powerful. She wondered if this was the end of any chance of repairing their relationship.

"You're right. I was not being very fatherly. I guess I wanted the best for you and when you stubbornly ignored our pleas, I just tossed up my hands and went about my business. I didn't expect it to go on so long." His voice tapered off, and a pinch of sadness rang through.

"Daddy. I forgive you."

There, she said it.

"Thank you, honey. Now can we come and see that grandson of ours?"

"Yes," she shouted. "Yes, please come."

"What do you mean the car disappeared?" Shelley's tone elevated.

"The crew went out in the lot to get her, to bring her in for a detail and she wasn't anywhere to be seen," Tom Flannigan said.

"That's awful. What am I going to do?"

"You didn't tell her about the car, right?" Tom asked.

"No, I didn't tell her about the car," Shelley said, irritated.

"Come back down and let's find her a new one. I have a lot of good ones that just came in as trade-ins."

"I can't right now. My parents are coming in for a visit from out of state. I have a birthday party to plan and a Thanksgiving dinner to prepare, and my store is hopping with early Christmas shoppers. This really puts a wrench in my plans to give it to her this week."

Except for some heavy breathing from Tom, it was silent.

"After my parents leave, I'll come by. That's all I can do."

"I did report the car stolen so if it shows up, I'll let you know."

"It will probably look like crap and not even a detail would make it shine again." Shelley's sarcastic tone shot through the phone.

"It was probably a bunch of teens looking to get into trouble," Tom said.

She realized she was being hard on him. It wasn't his fault.

"Let's just see what happens. Thanks for calling me. Have a happy Thanksgiving."

"You too. We'll find Jennie the perfect car for her and her family. This is too great of a cause for us not to," Tom said.

"I agree."

She dropped the phone onto the counter and leaned up against it, her hips hitting the hard granite. "Onward we go," she said, throwing up her hands.

She went back to her grocery list she'd been entering on her color note app. Turkey, check. Small boneless smoked ham, check. Sweet potatoes, check. Rolls, butter, check. Pies, whipped cream, check. Green beans, soup, dried onion rings, check. "Oh, cranberry sauce," she said. "I think that's it."

"Come on, Billy. We're off to the grocery store," she yelled.

"Are we getting stuff for my party?" He clasped his hands together as if he were praying.

"Yes, but we're also getting things for Thanksgiving dinner. What kind of cake do you want?"

"Chocolate," he yelled.

Shelley knew as soon as Billy saw the little cart, he'd want to push it along with her and the larger one. She'd let him help. She nodded over to it.

He ran and pulled it out of the stacked carts and waited for her as she grabbed the larger cart.

"Let's head over to the bakery and see what they have."

She usually would order a custom cake, but with her parents coming and the stress of preparing such a large meal, she was hoping there would be one in the case that would appeal to him.

She found a rectangular one with white icing that said Happy Birthday in blue frosting.

"This would work. Maybe we can ask the nice lady behind the counter to add your name and a car or something?" She leaned into the display case and retrieved the cake.

"I don't want a car."

"Okay. What then?" She rang the bell at the counter.

A young woman came from the corner and smiled.

"I was wondering if you could add his name to this cake? And I was hoping for some sort of design or candle or something to make it a bit more personalized. Any suggestions?"

"How old are you going to be?" The lady's gaze lowered to Billy.

He held up six fingers.

"I have the perfect thing."

She bent down and began rummaging through the cabinet. "Ta-da!" She held up a number six.

Billy grinned.

"What's your name?" She took the cake from Shelley.

"Billy," he said.

"Okay, Billy. And what do you like to do?"

"Well I do like to play cars, but I don't want that on the cake." He strummed his finger to his chin.

Shelley giggled.

"Football," he squealed.

She walked into the back of the bakery with the cake. While they waited, she shopped.

"Grab four cans of those," Shelley said, motioning to the green beans.

He picked up each can and rolled them into his cart. She moved along the aisle and tossed in the soup and some of the other items on her list. Billy added a few more items to his grocery cart, and when the shopping was done, they headed to the bakery to get the cake.

"I hope you like it," the baker said.

Shelley's eyes widened. She lowered the confectionary delight to Billy's eye level. He jumped up and down. "I like it," he said over and over.

She'd cleaned off the entire top of the cake and made it like it was a football field. She wrote Happy Birthday Billy in the middle, and in the top right-hand corner, she inserted the candle.

"Thanks again," Shelley said as they headed to pay for their goods.

He rose up on his tiptoes as he laid items on the conveyer belt. The clerk hit the button and made the items move toward her. When Shelley got ready to pay, she inserted her card into the card reader and entered her pin number.

"I'm sorry, but it said it's been declined," the clerk said. "Do you have another card to use?"

"That's impossible. I have money in there."

The clerk shrugged.

Shelley could feel her face turn hot. Embarrassed about the entire situation, she dug into her wallet and produced another card.

"I'm sorry, but that one has been declined too."

"Okay, wait a minute. There is no way both of those cards would be rejected. It's your card machine." Shelley lowered her voice when she realized everyone could hear her.

"I'm sorry, ma'am, but I haven't had any issues with that machine until you."

Shelley pulled out her wallet. She thumbed through her cash. She peered over to the register, to see the amount she owed. She was about fifty dollars short.

"I'll just have to go to the ATM machine and get cash. Please hold the groceries for me."

The lady started tossing the items back into the cart, and with a frown, canceled her order.

"I'll be right back," Shelley said.

She grabbed Billy by the hand and flew out of the store.

"Mommy, we forgot the cake and turkey," he said, trying to keep up with her.

"I know, Billy. Something happened, and it wouldn't let me pay for them. I have to get money from the ATM."

Shelley stared at the ATM screen for minutes. No funds available. Was this some cruel joke? Of course she had funds available. She dashed inside the bank with Billy in tow. Fortunately, it was dead inside, and she got up to the teller quickly.

"There's some mistake regarding my bank account. I was just humiliated at the grocery store because neither of my cards worked. Then I came here to the ATM, and it says no funds available. What in the world is going on?" She could feel her pulse quicken, and although she wasn't sad about anything, her eyes teared up.

"Let's take a look," the teller said.

She clicked around the screen with her mouse and then printed something. She pushed it over to Shelley to take a look at it.

"Does this look right to you?"

Shelley lowered her gaze. It showed plenty of money in both accounts. "Yes. So why was my card declined?"

"I don't know. Most likely, it was their card reader."

"I tried to tell her that. But then why did it say no funds available out at the ATM?"

"Probably the computer going through updates. Everything is in order."

"What about my credit card that didn't work? A coincidence too?" She narrowed her eyes.

"I don't know about your credit card. I can only confirm that your banking cards do have funds available for purchase. Plus, you have overdraft protection. Can I help you with anything else, Ms. Bennett?"

"No. That's all. Thank you."

"Have a wonderful holiday," the clerk said. "Next," she said, looking around Shelley.

Shelley moved out of the way and took Billy by the hand.

She headed right back to the store, but this time she went to the customer service desk.

"My card was declined here just a while ago. I went to the bank and verified funds are available, and they said it was your card reader. I was embarrassed and humiliated, and this is not how I wanted to start my Thanksgiving holiday." She broke down in tears and sobbed.

"Ms. Bennett. Please, don't be upset. These things happen," the manager said warmly.

"They don't happen to me." She sniffled. "I'm a single parent, a proud shop owner and my parents are coming for dinner," she wailed.

"Are they holding your groceries for you?" He led her toward the registers with his hand on her shoulder.

"I don't really know. I had frozen stuff in there, probably the whipped cream is all thawed out by now."

"Let's go see."

He waved over to one of the clerks.

"Did you ring up Ms. Bennett earlier?"

"Yes. Her card declined."

The manager put a finger to his lips to silence her from saying any more.

"She's gone to the bank, and everything is fine. Please ring her up on a different register. I'm going to have a technician look at the card reader."

"But—"

The manager held up a finger again. "Please just do as I ask."

A sniffling Shelley and wide-eyed Billy followed the young woman.

"I'll grab your cart. We were just getting ready to put things up."

This time her card went through without a hitch. But the damage was done. Exhausted by the day's events, Shelley and Billy treated themselves to a thick chocolate milkshake. Even on a cold November day, ice cream warmed the soul, and boy did she need it.

"Mommy, I love you. We're going to be okay."

The tears gushed out without any notice. Shelley wiped her face with a napkin.

"Don't cry, Mommy. We're having ice cream."

"We are," she said, choking back more tears. "And you know what else?"

He dipped his straw, then pulling it out, licked the creamy mixture. "What?"

"Your grandparents are coming for a visit!"

"They are?"

"Yes. I wanted to wait and tell you, but we need some good news about now. They'll be here in three days."

"Yippee." He yanked the straw back out of the cup and flung it, getting ice cream in Shelley's hair. "Sorry, Mommy." He giggled.

"No worries. Mommy isn't angry. She's having a great day."

They finished their midday treat and headed home. And when she remembered the whipped topping in the bag that was probably a blob of creamy white stuff, it didn't bother her a bit.

"Mommy, is Skip coming over for my birthday party?"

"I guess so. Actually, I hadn't asked him. I will, though."

"He's coming over tonight. You can ask him yourself."

He surprised them by bringing a large pepperoni pizza by. Shelley dug out the paper plates, and they sat around the living room, eating and laughing. With cheese dripping down his chin, Billy asked Skip about the party.

"I wouldn't miss it for the world, bud," he told him.

"I asked Mommy to make sloppy joes."

A small gasp exited Shelley's mouth when she recalled the episode the last time they had sloppy joes together.

"That sounds delicious," Skip said.

As if Billy realized they wanted to be alone, he jumped up from the floor. "I'm going to go play a game on my tablet," he announced.

After he bolted from the room, Skip placed his hands on her, kneading her tense muscles along her neck and shoulders. She melted into his strong hands. A soft moan escaped her lips. "That feels divine."

"Good. Just relax. Breathe in, let it out. Close your eyes and dream of fluffy marshmallows."

Shelley sat up and opened her eyes. "Fluffy marsh-mallows?"

"That's what my shrink tells me to think about when I'm scared or stressed. It works."

She leaned back into his arms. "How about fluffy whipped topping?"

"If that works for you, yes." He wrapped his strong arm around her. "I'm sorry you had such a rough day. First, Jennie's car is stolen, then your card wouldn't work at the store—"

"It wasn't my card," she interjected.

"Excuse me. The card reader." He chuckled before continuing. "What else bad happened?"

"Nothing. It's all good. Someone above is testing me, is all." She laid her head on his arm.

"You're testing yourself."

She turned slightly and locked eyes with him.

"You're testing yourself to see how much you can take, and how you react to it. It's all about reaction and then what we do with it. How we channel it and make a positive out of a negative."

"Wow. Your shrink is good. Maybe I need to go see her."

"She really is. I've been able to let go of so much baggage since I started seeing her. I still have some stuff to figure out, but man, I can finally see the light at the end of the tunnel." He leaned in and kissed her.

THE BIRTHDAY PARTY consisted of just Shelley, Skip, and Billy. She'd thought about inviting Jennie and her children, but with Thanksgiving a few days away, her parents coming and all the stress she felt from the upcoming visit, she decided against asking them, then felt awful later about not inviting them.

Skip surprised Billy with colorfully wrapped gifts. After dinner he opened them, expressing his happiness by hugging Skip. Shelley tried to hide the tears, but her heart was overjoyed, and having Skip there meant the world to her and to Billy.

While Billy played with the onslaught of new toys which included a tabletop football game, a Batman figure complete with a Batmobile, and various other toys, Shelley and Skip cozied up on the couch, sipping hot coffee while they watched him.

"So…my parents are going to be here in a couple of days. It's going to be emotional, stressful, and everything in between. You are coming to dinner, right?" She touched his fingertips with hers.

"Yes. I would much rather have turkey and all the trimmings here than at the soup kitchen."

"Even if it means meeting the parents?"

He closed his fingers around hers. "Even if it means meeting the parents." Leaning in, he brushed his lips over hers.

CHAPTER 19

Shelley stood back from the crowd while holding Billy's hand, never taking her eye off the sea of people moving along as they exited the airport. It'd been a long time, but she'd never forget what they looked like. Her father appeared first, then her mother. As they came closer into view, Shelley smiled. Except for a little weight around the middle, her father fared well. Her mom appeared to be thinner, her face sunken with stress lines across her forehead. Shelley wiggled her hand free from Billy. "There they are," she said, getting down to his level and pointing ahead. "That's your grandpa and grandma."

She popped her hand up into the air and waved madly. "Mom, Dad, over here."

"Oh honey," her mom cried out, embracing her, a rosy tint covering her cheeks.

"Dad," Shelley said, a bit reserved but with a hint of emotion in her voice.

He held out his arms, and she waltzed right into them, shedding a few tears before she got all into his warm bear hug. He kissed her on the cheek. "It's so good to see you." His eyes moved around her. "And this must be the little guy." He bent down and scooped him up into his arms and squeezed him so hard he giggled.

"Be gentle, Henry," Shelley's mother said.

"This little guy can take a lot, can't you?" Henry tickled Billy, making him laugh harder.

"There'll be plenty of time for roughhousing, you two. Let's get your luggage, shall we?" Shelley reached for Billy's hand. But Billy reached up and grabbed his grand-pa's hand instead. Her eyes began to water. Having male role models was so important for children. Especially little boys.

"I DON'T FEEL RIGHT about you giving up your room for us," Cora said as she dried dishes.

"It's okay. This couch is comfy." Shelley left off the part that she knew firsthand how comfortable it was. She'd spent many a night on it when she couldn't sleep and counting sheep in her dark bedroom did little to help her. "I don't mind at all." She flashed a grin.

"Do we need to do any shopping for Thanksgiving dinner?" Cora turned the attention to food.

"I think I've got everything. Thought we could go over the menu tonight after we get Billy to bed."

Shelley's folks sat in the living room while she got Billy ready for bed. She knew he'd have trouble falling asleep. It'd been a little overwhelming with meeting the grandparents he'd only dreamed about. She tucked him in and pressed her lips to his forehead.

"Mommy," he whispered.

"Yes." She stood looking over him.

"What are we going to do tomorrow?"

"Well, let's see. I thought we could take Grandpa and Grandma on a little sightseeing trip. Maybe stop into Lucy's diner and get lunch? How does that sound?"

"Good. Can we take them to the park? I want to show Grandpa how I can run and jump."

"That's a thought. We could. Let me ask them, okay?" She turned off the light. "Sleep tight. I love you."

Just then, Henry and Cora shuffled up to the door. "Can we say good night to him?" Henry asked.

"Well, of course. I'm sorry. We're not used to having anyone here but us." Shelley moved out of the way.

Cora flipped on the light and went to Billy's bedside. "Grandma loves you. We're so proud of you and your mom." She leaned over and kissed his cheek.

Henry cleared his throat as he sat on the edge of the bed. It bounced a little, and Billy laughed.

"I don't know what your mom has planned for us tomorrow, but I thought we could go to a park or something and toss a ball around. Would you like that?"

Billy reared straight up and hugged Grandpa's neck. Henry blinked a few times and then choking back tears, said, "I guess I'll take that as a yes."

Cora blew kisses, Henry gave him a big salute, and then the lights went out.

"Would anyone like a nightcap?" Shelley brought out the smoky amber liquid she saved for special occasions. Or in most cases, when she needed something to calm her down, soothe her soul.

"Sure, sounds good, hon." Cora took down three glasses from the cabinet. She'd already learned her way around Shelley's kitchen.

Shelley splashed a little in each glass and handed her mother hers. She moved to the living room where her dad was comfortable with his feet up on the coffee table. It made her happy he felt so at home. "Here, Dad."

He drew the short glass to his lips and tasted it. "Nice," he said.

The three of them sat around and chatted a bit, enjoying their time together. She and her mother went over the menu for Thanksgiving dinner. They agreed no one would go hungry.

"By the way, I wanted to let you know I've invited someone to have dinner with us. I hope you don't mind." Shelley swirled the liquid in the glass.

"Of course not, dear. This is your home," Cora said.

"Who is it?" Henry asked, getting right to the point.

"A friend. Actually, he works for me too. His name is Skip Morrison. He's a former army intelligence officer."

"Sounds serious," Cora said, with a twinkle in her eye.

"We're just figuring things out between us. Billy really adores him. He's kind and brave, and strong," she said, stopping after that.

"We'd love to meet him, Shelley," Cora said.

Henry stood and stretched. "Well, I better hit the hay, or this grandpa will be worthless to his grandson. Cora, you coming?" He headed to the kitchen to rinse out his glass.

"Yes, dear," she said. "I'm so happy we've put the past behind us, Shelley. We've been so sad about all of this. Too much time has gone on. We want to be a part of Billy's life." She leaned over and kissed Shelley on the cheek. "Good night, dear."

Shelley could hear low mumblings coming from her bedroom as they settled in for the night. The apartment was too small not to hear stuff. She slid off her jeans and pulled her top up over her head, slipping on an oversized tee-shirt and a pair of shorts. Fluffing up her pillows, she unfolded her blanket. Crawling under it, she soon fell asleep, and she didn't even have to count any sheep.

SHELLEY and her mother tag teamed breakfast. While her mother browned the sausage links, Shelley made up the pancake batter. After a hearty breakfast, they got ready for their first day out in Bozeman.

Her mother went on and on about how modern the town was. Shelley wondered what she expected. The wild west? Her father kept commenting on the traffic.

"Yes, we've kind of exploded here in Bozeman," Shelley said as she weaved through the line of snarled cars.

"I had no idea it was so popular," Cora said.

"When Billy and I moved here a few years ago, it was booming then, but it's gotten crazy. They're calling it Bozangelas," Shelley said.

"Why do people always do that?" Cora asked.

"Do what, Mom?"

"Ruin a good place."

"People are just trying to find a good place to settle down. Raise families with good schools. I don't blame them. But it does make it difficult sometimes to get around town. I usually park over by my shop and walk most places."

"Do we get to see this shop of yours?" Henry asked.

Shelley never closed the store, but she also never had anyone to help her. Now that business was booming, she knew she needed to find someone to help her. She had to be able to take some time off every once in a while. But with the Friday after Thanksgiving one of the biggest shopping days of the year, she had to work.

"I will give you a tour. Normally we're open, but I closed up so I could be with you all."

"That doesn't make good business sense, Shelley," Henry said.

"I know, but the shop was struggling before. I couldn't afford to hire anyone. Now, it's really doing well. I have a flyer up in the window. Hoping to hear something soon. Here we are," she said, pulling into the lot across the street.

"Look at the name of the store, Henry." Cora laced her arm in his. Shelley watched as her parents marveled at her shop's name. They seemed so much in love.

"It's catchy. A great name for a stationery shop," Henry said.

Billy ran up to the door and jiggled the knob. "It's locked."

"Yes. Mommy closed up the shop today." She inserted the key and opened the door.

As she flicked on lights, her parents explored the store with Billy leading the way. Shelley smiled when she heard him pointing various things out.

"I love it," Cora announced, puffing her chest out slightly. "It's cute, it's clever, it's just what this town needs."

"Thanks, Mom. That means a lot."

"All you need is some part-time help, and you'll be all set."

"I have an engraver now, so that's really helped me. In fact, that's what Skip does here. You're going to meet him tomorrow."

"I know it's probably a bit dead the day before Thanksgiving, but what about Friday? If you keep these doors closed, you're potentially missing out on sales," Henry said.

"I know. I think I'll have to work. I was hoping you guys could hang out with Billy?"

"Sure, honey. We'll do whatever you need."

"We can help, you know. I was a pretty good salesperson back in my day," Henry said, crossing his arms.

"We'll see, Dad. But thanks for offering. Okay so how about heading to the park and then grabbing lunch?"

CHAPTER 20

Shelley nervously watched the clock on the back of the stove. She and her mother were busily preparing the Thanksgiving feast, and although it did occupy her thoughts some, Skip Morrison occupied them more.

"I can't wait to meet your new fellow," her mom said as she peeled potatoes.

"I hope you like him. Billy and I do." Shelley opened the oven and basted the turkey.

"Something smells good," her dad yelled from the living room where he and Billy were putting a puzzle together.

"You mentioned he'd served our country. That's very honorable," her mom said.

Shelley wasn't sure how much to tell her about his past with the army. Some things were better left unsaid.

"Yes, he did. He doesn't like to talk about it a lot, though."

Her mother turned and rested her hips against the counter. "Oh?"

"He saw some stuff while stationed overseas."

Her mother blinked a couple of times. "What kind of stuff?"

"Mom, that's the part that is sensitive with him. Please let it go. You're going to like him, I promise." She turned away and began to put together the sweet potato casserole.

"I just know many of our soldiers have come back with trauma. PTSD, I think they call it."

"Post-traumatic stress disorder," Shelley said.

"Yes. It's a shame. And then the military medical community is not taking care of them as they should. I read that, as well."

Shelley relaxed her shoulders. This was going better than she'd expected.

"I hope he's getting the help he needs."

Just then a knock at the door had them both looking up. "He's here." Shelley grabbed a towel off the counter and wiped her hands.

Billy beat her to the door as always. Shelley felt more comfortable with him opening it with her folks there. He grabbed the knob and flung the door open. "Skip!"

"Hey there, buddy." He ruffled up Billy's hair. "You look nice." He winked at Shelley.

She felt the blood rush to her face. "Thanks. Come in."

"Skip, Grandpa and me are putting a puzzle together."

"Oh, cool."

"Want to help us?"

"Sure. In a minute." He made his way over to Cora and put out his hand. "Hi. I'm Skip Morrison."

"Nice to meet you. I'm Cora."

"And I'm Henry," her dad said, coming into the kitchen space with his hand out.

"Nice to meet you, sir."

"So, Shelley tells us you are a military man. Thank you for your service." Henry puffed out his chest as he tucked in his shirt. "I never went in. I have a hearing disability which wouldn't allow me to join."

"Sometimes I wished I hadn't gone in. But it is what it is."

"Dinner will be ready in about forty-five minutes. Just going to pop the sweet potato casserole into the oven and get started on boiling the potatoes for the mashed ones," Shelley said.

Glad Skip took the cue and went into the living room with Billy and her dad, Cora and she finished getting dinner ready. But she kept her ear stretched as far as she could, trying to pick up on the conversation in the other room.

AS THEY PASSED around the dishes, Skip studied Shelley and her parents' interactions. He trained with the army on picking up certain movements and mannerisms. He could pick out a stressful situation quickly. He was observant. It seemed pretty calm at the Bennett household. Some laughter, a bit of whimsical conversation, light and cheery with her dad throwing in a zinger every now and then. Normal. This was a normal holiday dinner.

"The dinner is delicious. My hat's off to both of you ladies," Skip said, tipping his head.

"Wait until you taste dessert," Henry said in between mouthfuls.

Skip leaned back and rubbed his stomach. "I don't know if I'll have room."

"Henry believes if you say the word dessert enough, your mind will tell your stomach to make room."

"Mind over matter," Henry said, snickering. "Works every time."

"Shelley tells us you two are involved in helping someone less fortunate. Get a car, right?" Henry forked a piece of turkey.

"Yes, but unfortunately someone stole it right out of the dealership lot."

"How does that happen?" Cora asked.

"They are kind of on the outskirts of town. Probably teens. But he'll find us another one. I'm just waiting until after the holiday, and then we'll pick out another."

Henry started coughing, his face turning beet red. Shelley and Cora cried out, "he's choking," and suddenly Skip pushed back his chair, knocking it over and moving quickly behind Henry. He yanked him, chair and all, back from the table, stood him up and wrapped his arms around his chest. Making a fist with one hand, he covered it with his free hand and performed several thrusts until the food dislodged, and he was able to talk.

"Are you all right?" Skip asked.

"Yes. Just a bit scared. I've never choked before."

"Daddy, are you all right?" Shelley's voice escalated.

"Henry, are you okay?" Cora said, coming to his side.

"Yes, I'm fine." He rested his hand over his heart. "My old ticker is beating so fast."

Billy stood by, clearly upset. "Grandpa, when I eat too fast or take too big of bites, I cough sometimes." Billy climbed onto his lap and laid his head on his chest.

"Sorry for the excitement, guys. Now back to normal programming," Henry said, trying to make light of the situation.

"I don't know if I can," Shelley said.

Skip reached out and clasped her trembling hands. "It's okay. He's fine. Let's finish our fantastic dinner you and your mom prepared."

Shelley smiled.

She took her seat, then Billy jumped off his grandpa's lap and returned to his seat. Cora slowly made her way to her chair. Skip sat last.

"I'm so thankful you were here," Cora said.

Skip took a couple of deep breaths and channeled his inner peace. He couldn't let them see it unnerved him a bit too. The army taught him that too. Never let them see you sweat.

After dinner, Shelley insisted he go into the living room with her parents and Billy while she made coffee and sliced pie. He waited until they all were settled into the other room before he sneaked a kiss.

"Skip," she whispered.

All that did was make him want her more. He kissed her again.

"I'm glad you feel so comfortable," she said, turning away.

"They might as well know right now. I'm crazy about their daughter." He rested his chin on her shoulder as she carefully slid out the slices to each plate.

He nibbled on her neck before pulling up. "Later."

HIS LOW GROWL made her tummy pitch and roll, along with a racing heartbeat. Her chest lifted as she took a deep breath, trying to steady her nerves, her emotions, her quivering body. She finished slicing and serving up the pie and then topped off the mugs with the hazelnut roasted coffee.

Skip stood and stretched. "I don't know about you all, but I sure could use some form of activity before I fall asleep in this comfy chair. Anyone up for a walk?"

"I am," Billy said, jumping up and down and waving his arms madly.

"Let me change into my sneakers," Cora said.

"Me too," Henry said. "I have weak ankles too. I don't want you saving me twice in one evening." He belted out a deep laugh.

The three of them sped away to get their shoes. Skip took the opportunity to steal another kiss. He slid his arms around her waist and held her. "Thanks for a great dinner and sharing your parents with me. I think things are going well between you guys." He rocked her in his arms.

"Yes. We're doing okay. They've missed a lot, but are working hard to make up for it."

He leaned in and kissed her softly

Letting her arms drop to her side, she enjoyed the softness of his lips.

"Ahem. Looks to me someone could use the shock of a cold breeze about now." Henry narrowed his eyes.

Refusing to answer him, she instead rushed to her room to retrieve her walking shoes.

"SHE REALLY CARES FOR YOU." Henry looked back toward the room.

"I care about her. And Billy." Skip was matter of fact.

"Good."

Skip rose up on his toes and then fell back flatly, crossing his arms. "Yeah, it is." He looked Henry squarely in the eyes when he said it.

CHAPTER 21

Skip held Shelley back and let her parents and Billy walk ahead. He'd take any opportunity to hold her hand and steal a little alone time. As alone as one can be with parents and son nearby. He muffled a laugh. "Your dad was right. The cool air is just what I needed." He squeezed her hand tight.

Feeling giddy with hope and desire, she swung his hands up and down. "I think we all needed it." She drew his arm close to her body and with her other hand, held it there. "Skip?"

"Uh-huh?"

"Are we going to make it?"

"Of course. Why do you ask?"

"Statistics show single moms with kids don't always find true love. Guys see them as having baggage."

"Where did you read that?"

"I didn't read it anywhere. I live it."

"That's all going to change. I want to be with you. I'm not going anywhere." He picked up their paired hands and kissed hers.

Henry and Cora managed to keep up with Billy. They found a bench at the park, and as they sat, Henry grunted and rubbed his stomach. "I'm so full," he said.

"Watch me, Grandpa," Billy yelled as he went down the slide.

Other families were enjoying the cool late afternoon and walking off their dinner. Shelley and her mom made small talk and wished them a happy Thanksgiving. Shelley looked over her shoulder and watched as Skip and her dad talked and laughed. Pulling her sweater to her, she hugged her arms. This was the best Thanksgiving in a long time.

"I'll be right back. Just going to walk Skip out to his truck."

"Good night, Skip," Henry called.

"It was a pleasure meeting you," Cora said.

Billy ran up and hugged Skip's leg. "See you, partner."

Skip messed up Billy's hair and made him laugh. "Not again," Billy screamed.

They walked slowly to the truck, enjoying their moment alone. The evening temperature had dropped. Shelley rubbed her arms.

Skip instinctively wrapped his arm around her, pulling her close. "How long did you say they are staying?"

"Through the weekend. They offered to help me run the store. Dad says it would be dumb for me to close during one of the busiest shopping weekends—but you still have the weekend off. No engraving. You rest and enjoy your time off. Sleep in late, take a hike, go see a movie. Relax."

"Relax while you're working hard. That doesn't seem very manly."

"I plan to put Mom and Dad to work. It'll be fine." They reached his truck.

He leaned up against the door, crossing his legs at the ankle. She couldn't imagine a sexier guy than Skip. She played with the ends of her hair, trying not to be obvious she was drooling over how gorgeous he was. What she wanted to do was leap into his arms and give him a kiss that took his breath away. Instead, she tried not to concentrate on his looks and demeanor, and calm her aching desire to do just that.

"But you are welcome to stop by if you are bored." She giggled.

"Come here," he said.

Her knees wobbled as she stepped forward.

He opened his arms wide. She walked into them as he embraced her. He dropped a kiss on the top of her head. "I can't wait to get you *alone* alone. Is that bad for me to say?"

"I don't know, is it? I mean, what would you do with me alone?" she teased him.

"Don't mess with me, Shelley. I'm so hungry for you I can hardly resist. I can't put it in words."

She gulped. The intensity was real. Her heart lurched, and her breath caught as he ran his fingers through her hair.

"Is it too soon?" he asked.

She smoothed her hands over his strong, protective arms. "I don't think so. The heart knows what it wants."

"I know what I want," he said, pulling her into his arms.

Her eyes fluttered closed. Her mouth dry as the desert, and her veins hot and throbbing like lava crawling down the side of a volcano, she waited. His finger traced her lips, causing a deepening of desire, and now her entire body was engulfed in flames. She reached up and laced her arms around his neck, holding him firmly. The warm sweetness of his breath drew her in, and the thumping of her heart, now ringing in her ears along with the longing in the pit of her stomach gnawing at her wildly, she grew more impatient. "Kiss me," she demanded.

She watched him as he drove off, happy for the few more moments in the crisp fall night to help her cool down. She had no idea where this thing was headed, but if he was right and true in what he said, they'd be together for the next Thanksgiving, and every holiday in between and after. She waited until she couldn't see the taillights any longer, then headed back inside. She hadn't realized she'd been gone so long. Cora had the entire kitchen cleaned up, Billy had a bath, and Grandpa was reading a bedtime story.

"Oh, hey, sorry about that," she said, embarrassed.

"No worries. We have it under control. We have a busy day ahead, so we think we'll turn in too." Cora leaned over and kissed Shelley on the cheek.

"Thank you, Mom."

Cora raised her brow. "For what?"

"For making all this happen. Coming out to Montana for Thanksgiving. For making Billy so happy. All of it." She lowered her gaze to the floor.

Cora raised Shelley's chin with the tip of her finger. "Honey. We all made it happen. That's what families are for. To love, support, lift us up when we fail, pat us on the back when we are successful. You've done a magnificent job raising Billy. Couldn't be any prouder. He's a good boy. You have a nice apartment, a budding career as an entrepreneur, and a handsome guy who I can tell really cares about you."

A tear rolled down Shelley's cheek.

"Don't cry, honey. We're on the fast train moving forward now."

"I know. I just can't help it. So much time passed. It was stupid how we let our feelings keep us apart."

"Let it go, Shelley. If you don't, it will eat you up. I had to. I can't go back. I won't."

Shelley nodded, drawing her shoulders up. "Right. We won't. Only forward. Tomorrow is a big day. I'll set the coffee pot to auto. I usually grab something from the bakery on the way into work. They have the best bagels."

"Okay, dear. Good night." Cora pressed a kiss to Shelley's forehead.

Shelley filled the carafe with water and dumped it into the back of the coffee maker. She got out the large thermos mugs and set them nearby. She cut the lights off and moved into the living room where her mother had already made up her bed. "Wow. I must have been outside with Skip longer than I thought." She stripped off her clothes, pulled on her night shorts and tee, and climbed under the cover. The face of her phone lit up, and so did her smile.

"Hey you," she whispered as she snuggled deeper under the covers.

"I couldn't go to bed without hearing your voice."

"I came back inside, and Mom had the kitchen cleaned. Dad had Billy in bed and reading him a story. We had a little chat too. We're putting all the wasted time behind us. No more living in the past."

"Good. That's what I have to do. Move forward. Each dawn brings a new day. We have to make the most of it."

"Yeah, we do."

"Listen, I have to tell you something," Skip said.

Shelley pulled up and rested her back against the pillow. "Oh?"

"I've never had any woman, ever, make me feel the way you do."

"What about your wife?"

"Nope. Not even her."

"How can that be?" Shelley asked.

"I didn't know it at the time. I loved her. No doubt about it. But after she left me and made a mess out of my life, I got to thinking about stuff. We hadn't been happy in a while. She probably did us both a favor by jumping ship."

She leaned her head back and looked up into the darkness.

"And, I'd never have found you if I stayed with her, or she with me."

"You have a valid point, Skip. I was crushed Billy's dad didn't want us. But if he had, my life and Billy's would have been miserable. And then I wouldn't have found you."

"We found each other when we both needed it the most," Skip said.

"I know I told you to relax this weekend. But if you can spare a few minutes, I'd love to see you."

"Are you kidding?"

"I know. I shouldn't be so selfish. I gave you the time off. I'm sorry. I'll see you next week."

"No. I mean, are you kidding? You couldn't keep me away!"

A gush of air poured out of her lungs.

"Shelley?"

Choking back the emotion that lodged in her throat, she squeaked out, "Yes."

"This is going to be the best Christmas ever. I can't wait to see the look in Jennie's eyes when we present her with the car, I can't wait to see Billy's eyes light up when we go chop down the tree and decorate it, and mostly, I can't wait to kiss you under the mistletoe."

"You're going to make me cry, Skip."

"What's wrong with a few tears?"

"My eyelids will be all puffy tomorrow. I can't have that."

"Go get some ice and wrap it in a towel. Place it on your eyes for about twenty minutes."

"You have the cure for everything, don't you?"

"I may have cures for choking dads and swollen eyes of girlfriends, but you have the cure for my lonely heart."

And with that, tears trailed down her cheek.

AFTER AN EXHAUSTING BLACK FRIDAY, the four of them decided although the fridge had mountains of leftovers, no one wanted to lift a finger to put anything together. So, upon Billy's urging, they ordered a pizza to go.

"I thought Skip was coming by." Cora helped herself to a slice.

"Yeah, I thought so too," Shelley said, a bit worried.

"He probably got busy doing something. You know those army guys. They can't rest for a minute." Henry took a small bite of his pizza and chewed carefully.

"I'll call him later. Just to make sure everything is okay. I'm exhausted." Shelley took her plate into the living room and propped her feet up on the coffee table.

But when she called him, it went to voice mail. Every time. All night.

CHAPTER 23

The weekend rolled around and still no Skip. She'd left at least a half dozen messages on his phone. When she went to leave the last one on Sunday evening, it said his mailbox was full. Not wanting to admit he'd done it again to her and Billy, Shelley tried to not think about him and instead kept busy helping her mom pack for their trip back home.

"I thought for certain we'd see Skip again before we took off," Cora said, folding a pair of slacks neatly and laying them in the suitcase.

"He wanted me to apologize to you both, but something came up."

"What came up?" Cora asked.

Not enjoying the fact she was telling her mother a bald-faced lie, Shelley turned slightly away from her. "He's helping an old army buddy."

"It must be something very important."

"Of course it is." Shelley lowered her gaze to her watch. "We better hurry up. Don't want you missing your flight."

A few tears fell as she bid her parents goodbye. She couldn't determine if it was because the visit was over with, glad that the visit was over with, or because Skip dropped off the face of the earth. Probably a combination of all of them. It'd been an exhausting few days, and now with the holiday shopping in full swing, it would only get worse. Orders were beginning to back up for engraving. Damian would be overwhelmed after coming back from his holiday break.

"Mommy, where is my buddy Skip?" Billy played with his shoestrings, not making eye contact with her.

She began to utter another lie but stopped. "I don't really know, Billy."

"He might be dead."

Shelley widened her eyes and dropped her jaw. "Dead? Why would you say that?"

"Because why wouldn't he be here then?"

Shelley placed her arm around Billy's shoulders. "I'm sure he had a good reason. Let's go home and have warmed-up turkey sandwiches for dinner. We have to get to bed early tonight. School and work tomorrow."

While Billy played with Legos, Shelley warmed up their dinner. Opened-face sandwiches piled high with turkey and stuffing, smothered in gravy. Comfort food at its best. And she needed it to drown out her sorrow.

They sat in silence as they ate their dinner. Her sadness turned to anger then back to sorrow, making her throat tighten and difficult to enjoy her dinner. Her eyes began to mist, and then the tears came.

"What's wrong, Mommy?"

She pushed her plate away. "I'm just tired."

Billy finished his dinner and slurped down his milk. "Can I watch cartoons?"

"Yes, for a little bit. Then you need to jump in the tub."

She cleaned up the kitchen while he watched TV. She tried to keep her mind clear of Skip Morrison. She didn't wish him to be dead, but it would be an explanation. Shaking her head, trying to clear the cobwebs, she went back to washing and rinsing the dishes.

She went through the motions during bath time with Billy. While he soaked and played in the tub, she sat on the edge dazed and confused. Her short answers of yes, no, and uh-huh went unnoticed to him, or so she thought. She studied the bookcase long and hard. All the titles seemed to run together. Her heart wasn't in it to read to him. Darn Skip Morrison.

"Mommy, you can skip the book tonight. What you need is a bubble bath."

She whirled around and flashed him a wide grin. Did he know what he was saying? Did he realize he just picked her up off the floor? She rushed over to the bed and bounced next to him. "I love you. You know that, right?" She nuzzled noses with him.

"Yes, Mommy," he said, giggling.

"I have something to tell you about Skip."

It came over her like a dark cloud. The words spewed out without any warning. The truth. It always came out.

"What? Is he dead?" Billy's eyes consoled her.

"I don't think so. But I don't know."

A ringing noise came from the living room. "Your phone, Mommy! It's Skip. He's not dead."

The ringing persisted. She knew she only had a couple seconds before it would go into voice mail. Could it really be him?

"Go," Billy said, pushing her arm.

Shelley leaped from the bed and sprinted down the short hall. "Hello." She breathed heavily into the receiver. The phone was dead.

Hanging her head low and dragging her feet, she moved toward Billy's room. Shaking her head slowly, she sat back on the edge of the bed. "It wasn't him. Probably a wrong number. Listen, we were okay before Skip. We'll be okay after him. I don't want you worrying about him any longer." She pecked a kiss on his cheek. Turning off his bedside light, she watched him as he settled under the covers. "Good night, Son."

Squirting entirely too many bubbles into her drawn bath, Shelley disrobed and stepped into the sudsy water. Resting her head on the cold porcelain tub, she closed her eyes. She'd given her heart to him. Fell for him like she said she wouldn't. Now she had a child in the other room thinking his buddy was dead, and she wishing he were.

SHELLEY WAITED for Damian before she turned the Closed sign around. A staff meeting was called for, even though they were just a staff of two. She went over in her head what she was going to tell him.

"That doesn't sound like something Skip would do," Damian said with a puzzled look.

"I agree. However, what else can I think? No phone calls, no messages, nothing."

Damian paced the shop, his hands dug deep into his pockets. "Did you call the police? Report a missing person?"

Shelley frowned. "No, I didn't. I don't know he's a missing person."

"He was going to come over to your house for dinner, and he never showed. You don't think that's a bit suspicious?"

Shelley bit down on her bottom lip. "I suppose. But he's kind of different. He's used to being on the road. How do I know he didn't decide to leave again?"

She couldn't believe how much she was telling him. Why would he care about their love life?

"I know Skip thought the world of you and your kid. He wouldn't just ditch you guys. I could bet my life on that." Damian tipped his head a few times. "No, something has happened. If you don't call the police, I will." He marched over to the shop phone and picked it up.

"I'd like to report a missing person."

SHELLEY WASN'T in the mood to look at cars, but a promise was a promise. Tom apologized over and over about the stolen car. Shelley didn't hold him responsible. Things happened. Look at her and Skip.

"This is a cute car," she said, touching the hood of a blue four-door.

"Low mileage, new tires, and believe it or not, a little old lady owned it."

Shelley peered at him through half-closed lids and smiled. "Driven by the old lady sales pitch, huh? Couldn't get more creative than that?" she snickered.

"No, Scouts' truth." He held up two fingers.

She pulled open the door and peered inside. "Leather upholstery?" She moved her hand across the buffed tan material.

"Yes, and did I tell you low mileage?" He dipped his hands into his pockets and rocked back on his heels.

She peered over the headrests into the back seat. "No holes. The interior looks spotless."

"It was garage kept."

"What else do you have?" Shelley asked.

"I have two others I can show you which may work."

After Shelley looked at the others, they both agreed the blue sedan was the best choice.

"Now, this is a really sweet car. I could probably get fifteen grand for it, easy. But a deal is a deal. I want to help Jennie out. So, you give me half that, and I'll donate the rest."

Shelley tossed him a sharp look. "That will leave twenty-five hundred dollars. I wanted to give her more. You know, so she could pay in advance for car insurance and get car seats for the little one."

"I'd planned on giving her the car, but things have been a bit slow around here. I have staff salaries to pay out. Tell you what. You give me five thousand for the car, and it's yours. Deal?" He pulled out his hand for a shake.

She shook his hand and smiled. "Deal."

Shelley didn't want to take any chances on this car, so she paid Tom the money, got the keys, and asked Damian to fetch the car. She coordinated with Quincy to pass the word around about the delivery of the car. She picked the date and time and knew Quincy would make sure the townspeople showed up. Getting Jennie there might prove to be more difficult.

She barely could keep up with the amount of traffic coming into the store each day. Convinced more than ever she needed more sales help, Shelley created another Help Wanted sign. This time she'd make sure not to fall for any drifters. She needed reliable employees.

"Shelley," Damian said.

She looked up with the marker in her hand. "I'm biting the bullet. I need more help."

"Good. Listen. I know where Skip is."

CHAPTER 24

After a long moment, Shelley found the words. "Are you one hundred percent certain it's him?"

"Yes. They found him at the bottom of a ravine."

"How badly is he hurt?" A touch of caring seeped into her voice.

"Bad. I think they said several broken bones."

She turned away from Damian. "So that's why he wasn't able to call me. He'd fallen." Her voice drifted off.

"The sheriff said he was dehydrated, and possibly suffered some memory loss. Do you want to go see him?"

"Where is he?"

"VA hospital."

SHELLEY CLOSED the shop and Damian drove them to the hospital. Images of him lying in a hospital bed flitted in and out of her mind. When they entered the facility, she was immediately overcome with the smell of disinfectant. The buildup of wax on the aged linoleum had a yellow tint. Stark white walls with rows of paned windows lined the long hall. The sounds of shoes tapped and the hushed tones of people wandering the halls reminded her why she wasn't particularly fond of hospitals.

Damian hit the button to the elevator. "He's on the fourth floor."

When they entered the next hall, they were on the floor where Skip was. The nurses at the station were busy, but Shelley was able to catch the eye of one and smiled.

"Can I help you?"

"We're here to see Skip Morrison."

"Room 420."

Damian and Shelley found the room, and both stopped outside the door. "This is going to be so hard," he said.

She nodded then placed her hand on the chrome door handle and pulled.

The first bed was empty. Her gaze traveled to the next bed near the window. Legs in casts and slung in a stirrup and soft moaning stopped her from continuing. She grabbed Damian's hand. "Skip."

"Yes," he said, shaking her loose.

She watched with a careful eye as Damian proceeded. He waved her to follow.

When her gaze landed on the badly bruised and bandaged man, she gasped. "Oh, Skip," she cried, lunging toward the bed, cradling his face and kissing him. "I'm so sorry I thought the worst about you. I love you."

A small flicker of movement in his eyes and then he lifted a few fingers, dropping them suddenly.

A doctor came in with the whoosh of his white coat as he rounded the bed. "I'm Dr. Fields. Are you family?"

"No. I'm his." She paused. "Girlfriend."

"He's pretty broken up. A broken leg, a broken pelvis, two broken ribs, a fractured wrist, and a bad concussion." The doctor pulled the chart off the hook and began flipping through pages. "His vital signs are good. He's drinking sips of water. We'll remove the catheter tomorrow and get him up. Physical therapy is scheduled for tomorrow morning."

"But he'll be all right, right?" Shelley wiped the tears away.

"I think so. He's in really good shape."

"Shelley."

"Yes, dear," she said, turning her attention back to Skip. "You shouldn't probably exert yourself."

"I'm sorry," he whispered.

"You don't have anything to be sorry about."

"Dinner."

"Shh," she replied, putting her fingers to his lips. "It's all forgotten. You just get better."

The doctor moved back near Skip, looking at his pupils with a light.

"I told you it wasn't like Skip to run out on you. I just knew something bad had happened."

"You were right. I should have known it too. But it's all so complicated."

"It's complicated all right, but he told me how he feels about you and the kid. He's been struggling with a lot of stuff, but he told me he never believed in anything so much as he believed in being with you."

"Now you're making me feel like a bad person, Damian."

"No, not at all. I get it. You've been burned. Can I guarantee one hundred percent he won't get spooked and run? Nope. But if I were a betting man, I'd say he's pretty happy and even during those days when he feels the need to escape, if you give him a little breathing room to figure things out, he'll be right back in your corner."

"You're such a little old man, Damian! So wise. Beyond your years, really." Shelley looped her arm around his.

The doctor finished examining Skip, then briefed them both. "If he continues to mend this fast, I expect him to be up and around in a couple of days. We'll be testing him on his cognitive skills as well. Why don't you come back tomorrow?"

Damian drove them back into town. "I have everything arranged. Jennie and the kids will be in the town square a week from tomorrow."

"Skip should be there with us. After all, he made it happen with his huge donation," she said.

Damian chuckled. "He's a strong dude. He might just surprise you."

SHELLEY WRUNG her hands in anticipation of Jennie's surprised look. She hadn't been this nervous since Skip kissed her. The car was hidden out of sight, and the plan was, Damian would drive it around and park it right in front of Jennie and the kids, hopping out and handing her the keys. The crowd would erupt in applause and cheers, and there wouldn't be a dry eye in sight.

The crowd began to gather around the decorated gazebo in the town square. The twinkling white lights glistened against the backdrop of snow. A fresh layer of powder coated the grounds and hung graciously on the shingles. People were wrapped up in their winter garb. Billy was dressed head to toe in warm layers, the wool-lined ear flaps to his hat snugly covering his ears. Shelley zipped up her coat and pulled up her hood, securing it in place and tied it under her chin. The wind kicked up, and she shuddered from the cold. She worriedly looked at her watch. Christmas carols played in the background as the mayor and other administrators huddled under the gazebo, waiting for their moment. It'd all been rehearsed. Damian would drive the car out in sight when he heard the music cued. But then, when does anything ever go as rehearsed?

The loud sound of cymbals shook the sounds of winter out of a slumber. Shelley turned as all the people did, looking toward the sound. Soon, a marching band appeared with drums tapped, trumpets blaring, and then on the count of the leader, they broke into a Christmas song. This wasn't good. How'd Damian know when to drive the car around?

Shelley dashed in between the crowds, making her way around the back. Just then someone tapped the mic, making a loud, squelching noise. "Can I have your attention please?"

Shelley's heart jackhammered. She knew that voice.

"Thank you, everyone, for coming out today on this cold, blustery day. It's a special occasion. We're not only celebrating the start of the holiday season, but we're also honoring someone in the crowd today."

Shelley made her way toward the front and locked eyes with Skip. Standing with crutches, his wrist bandaged to his elbow, and bruises still showing, he flashed a wide grin down at her.

Her stomach pitched and rolled. Air whooshed from her lungs as she grasped what was taking place. His dreamy expression melted her heart, and for a moment, she considered fleeing the scene, but not to run away from him, but to join him on the stage.

"Everyone has a special someone in their life. Someone who makes them want to get up each day and meet the world head-on. Take the bumps along the way, but be better for it later. Someone to take a chance on you when others would not."

Shelley's eyes began to well up.

"That special someone is Shelley Bennett." He wobbled on his crutches a bit then held out his arms. "Come on up here, Shelley, and bring Billy."

Billy ran up the steps and got to him before she could. Her shoes heavy like cement, she finally made it up to the stage.

Skip turned slightly toward her. "Shelley," he said, his voice not wavering.

She nodded.

"I want to openly thank you for taking a chance on me. You gave me a job when I so desperately needed one. You showed me you cared, and I'll never forget it."

"You're welcome," she uttered softly.

"But let's not take up any more time about us. The folks want to see something nice, don't you?" he yelled into the mic.

"Kiss her," someone from the crowd yelled out.

"Ask her to marry you," another voice shouted.

"Now, now, folks. Calm down. I've said my piece. It's Shelley's turn."

Just then the music started playing the song they'd rehearsed this special moment for. She knew she only had a few seconds before Damian would drive the car out.

"Thank you all for coming tonight and braving this cold, but beautiful snowy evening. You all know our very sweet neighbor and friend, Jennie, who lost her husband. She's been without a car for quite some time." Shelley shielded her eyes from the lights as she searched the crowd for Jennie.

Jennie had a bewildered look as she wrapped her arms around her children, pulling them close.

"Jennie dear, we wanted to do something nice for you and the children."

Just then Damian came out driving and honking the horn of the blue sedan with a big red bow on the roof. Shelley met Jennie's eyes and smiled.

Damian jumped out of the car and dangled the keys. "This is for you."

The crowd clapped and cheered and watched as Jennie took the driver's seat and her children piled into the car.

"We'd like to thank Tom Flannigan for his gracious contribution toward this lovely car. And because we know car insurance is expensive, as well as other things like car seats, we also have a check made out to Jennie for five thousand dollars. We couldn't have done it without the folks here in Bozeman and our own Skip Morrison." She turned and clapped at him.

The band kicked in and started playing Christmas songs, making Shelley feel a bit melancholy. But this holiday season would be different. Her parents were back in the picture, Billy was thriving more than ever, and her business was growing by leaps and bounds—so much so that she had to hire another helper. And then there was Skip. Skip Morrison who drifted in her store one day with a glint in his eyes, a dashing grin, and his duffel bag clinging to him containing all his worldly possessions, looking for a job. Oh yes indeed, this would be a totally different Christmas.

"Zoom zoom," Billy said as he played with his metal cars on the living room floor.

Skip and Shelley cuddled on the sofa while drinking hot cocoa. He looped his free arm around her shoulder. He winced.

"Skip, remember, you're still healing," she said, scolding him gently.

"I'm fine." He leaned over, stealing a kiss.

"So, tell me again how you thought I ran off." He nudged her shoulder with his.

"I know I was being my insecure, crazy self."

"I told you I wasn't going anywhere. I didn't take into consideration falling into a giant hole." He chuckled.

"You never did tell me what you were doing up there on the ridge that day."

"Remember when we had our picnic up there? Billy almost got bit by a snake."

"How could I forget."

"In my haste to protect him, I lost something valuable to me. I went back up there to look for it."

She knitted her brows.

He loosened his arm from around her and dug into his pocket, pulling out a chain. He dangled it, showing off the cross.

"It's beautiful. But not sure it was worth risking your life for."

"This cross protected me every day while I was fighting a war. It helped me make it through my lowest moments after I got back and found out my wife left me, it brought me to your shop that day, and it helped me save Billy that day, but it saved me the day I fell too. I could have easily died right there. It's more than just a chain with a cross. It's helped me so many times." He clutched it in his hand, his eyes misting.

"I see," she softly said.

"Let me help you put it on." She held her palm open.

"Skip, want to play with me?" Billy called as he rolled his cars up and down the back of the couch.

"Sure, Son."

Shelley watched as the two played together. Happy to be together again, she looked up to the ceiling and mouthed the words, *thank you*, while wiping the few stray tears managing to roll down her cheek.

"Come on, Mommy. Play with us," Billy yelled.

Shelley dropped to her knees and grabbed a car. She rolled it up Skip's leg where he stopped it by placing his hand on it. He pulled her close and kissed her.

Billy started laughing. "Skip kissed Mommy," he said.

Shelley fanned her hot face.

"It's okay, Mommy. I like Skip. He makes us both happy. Go ahead and kiss him."

Shelley and Skip roared with laughter.

"That kid of mine, he's so grown."

"You can say that again." He pulled her close, their mouths millimeters apart. Raising his brows, he tipped his chin toward Billy. "He gave us permission."

She nodded.

Their lips touched, and her heart filled with love. Something she never knew would come to her again.

EPILOGUE

*J*ust as Skip promised, he took Billy and Shelley out to cut down a Christmas tree. She watched as he slid the saw back and forth at the trunk line, his muscles bulging even under his red-checkered flannel shirt. They took it home and decorated it with homemade popcorn strings, paper decorations Billy made in school, and a few glass ornaments she'd fallen in love with from the shop. As they sat back on the well-worn but comfy couch, admiring their work, Billy crawled under the tree to place the skirt.

"We need presents, Mom."

"Yes, we do," she said softly, enjoying the magical moment.

Low hanging branches brushed across his head as he slowly crawled out from under the tree. He ran over to them and bounced in between them. Looking first at his mom then to Skip, he took each of their hands into his. "I love you guys," he said.

"I love you," Shelley answered, squeezing his little hand.

"I love you, too, bud." Skip took their clasped hands and raised them up. "Tomorrow we'll go outside and toss the football around. Maybe go to the park and check out the remote-control plane you got for your birthday."

"That would be awesome," Billy sang out.

"What about me?" Shelley pursed her lips, her eyes twinkling at her favorite two guys.

"This is just a guy thing, Mom. You understand, right?" Billy's grown-up voice resonated deep.

Shelley looked over his little head and made eye contact with Skip. They both laughed.

"Kids. They say the darndest things," Skip said, then leaned and began tickling Billy.

"Yeah, and they are up way past their bedtime," Shelley said, tickling Billy on the other side.

"I get the message. I'm going to bed so you guys can kiss." He jumped off, but first giving Shelley a hug, then Skip.

They watched him as he traipsed off to bed.

"We have to watch that little old soul." Skip moved over closer to Shelley.

"We have to watch. I like the sound of that." She laid her head on his shoulder.

"I told you. I'm not going anywhere." He dropped a kiss on her head and then snuggled her deeper into his hold. "I'm through running. I've found my place."

"I'm through running too," Shelley said, looking up at him. "I love you, Skip."

He moved slightly out from her and studied her hard, making her wonder if she said the three words too fast. There was no taking them back. Besides, she meant them.

"I love you too. I love you, I love Billy, I love my life here in Bozeman," Skip said.

"I never knew I could be so happy, Skip. I know I put a wall up initially. It was just to protect Billy and me."

"I put the wall up. I was worried about so many things."

"The important thing is, we pushed through all of that and we're together."

"It won't be easy. I have a way to go with my rehabilitation, but if you and Billy stand by me, I know I can get through it."

Her eyes began to tear up. "I'm not leaving."

"Good. That makes two of us."

"No, that makes three of us," a tiny voice said from behind the couch.

A USA Today bestselling author, Debbie writes sweet contemporary romance and women's fiction. She lives in South Carolina with her husband and two dachshund rescues, Dash and Briar. She loves to hike, work in the garden, and on most sunny days you can find her enjoying her backyard. She's an avid supporter of animal rescue, and as such, pledges to happily donate a percentage of all book sales to local and national rescue organizations. When you purchase any of her books, you're also helping animals.

To find out more about Debbie, check out her website at https://www.authordebbiewhite.com

Ties That Bind

Passport To Happiness

The Missing ingredient

The Salty Dog

The Pet palace

Billionaire Auction

Billionaire's Dilemma

Coaching the Sub

Christmas Romance – Short Stories